"I'm afraid I recognize myself in at least one of these stories."

- Abigail Critchley

"New stories without computers, trolls, or little green men. A breath of fresh air!"

- Morris Quint

"Don't expect me to travel with you."

- The author's mother

This is a work of fiction. Any resemblance to persons living or dead would be very difficult to prove without severe embarrassment or imprisonment.

Cover photograph by Mimadeo. Cover design by Bespoke Designs, Yelverton, Devonshire.

ISBN: 9798482366356

Clubs, Bills and Partisans

Tales of Yet More Undivulged Crimes

by

Michael Reidy

Lattimer & Co.

PHILADELPHIA • PARIS

2021

For Françoise

Clubs, bills and partisans! Strike! Beat them down! Down with the Capulets! Down with the Montagues!

- *Romeo & Juliet*, I, i

Foreword

Do we learn from an early age to focus on a specific "reality" and filter out everything else for the rest of our lives?

Is that why some people appear to display extraordinary abilities and talents? Have they focused on a different reality?

The tales here may suggest that some have. All I am certain of is that the more I listen, the more stories I hear of lives that bear little resemblance to my own.

For readers of my other stories, there are more "Westbury Tales" here. "The Holly Ball" follows the events of "The Hayride," published in *Thoughts and Whispers*, while "The Valentine's Hop" relates the further lives of the characters found in both.

In June 2020, the masterful story teller, Carlos Ruiz Zafon, died, too young, at age fifty-five. "City of Spirits" is an homage to the enchanting myth he created in his wondrous and beloved city of Barcelona.

October 2021
Paris

Clubs, Bills and Partisans

The Holly Ball
A Westbury Tale

Clubs, Bills and Partisans

The Holly Ball
A Westbury Tale

Winter 1966

Sally Hawes had had a good week. No, it had been a great week. She had said goodbye to her cousin from Arizona who had been with her for weeks and weeks, and she had bought a *gorgeous* dress for the Holly Ball.

Getting rid of Josie took an enormous weight off her mind. Her constant talk of horses, ranches and what her school was like back in Cowpat County was compounded by the never-ending blare of Buck Owens and his Buckaroos. Sally liked a good western as much as anyone else, but at least in a good western you got to shoot someone.

There *had* been the episode at the Hayride last week. She had definitely said some things she shouldn't have. They needed saying, she told herself, but it may have been the wrong time and place.

What surprised her most was lack of support from her supposed friends. They seemed to like Josie and saw her as something more than a quaint form of alien life from some place no one would ever want to go. She'd even had dates and people laughing at her jokes, not at her.

As for the Patricia Detweiler business – well, she'd had that coming for a long time. Her family was on the way down, no matter how many millions they'd had in previous generations; the steel industry around Westbury was finished. Why her friends reacted the way they did was unexpected. Who would have thought that mousy girl would have so many people who liked her? No one had ever said so before, Sally thought.

Still, she had apologized, and would no doubt, do so again. Sally continued to think her assessment of things was right even though no one else did. Sometimes it was hard to be the only one who could see things clearly. Still her position was secure despite this minor setback. Tom would escort her to the Holly Ball, and she could hold court again.

ഌ

Pinehill School's Holly Ball was second only to a prom in social importance. The girls reckoned that if they played things right at the Holly Ball, they'd have a date for the Valentine Hop, and would secure an invitation to a decent prom at a boys' school in May.

For that reason, Pinehill didn't have its own prom. For the school, it was a lot less hassle to arrange two lower key dances than to deal with the expense and trauma of a prom.

The Holly Ball was, in fact, more elegant than most proms. With traditional Christmas trees, wreaths, lights and laurel swags along with a log fire in the hall's nineteenth century fireplace, it was more stylish than the tackier attempts at creating faraway places with cardboard and paint at most proms.

Girls would invite boys to these two dances, but it would be up to them to generate an invitation to a prom. The two most desirable ones to attend were the ones at the Academy and St. Benedict's. They carried equal kudos. As these dances were held on the same night, there was no chance of attending both.

The proms at the two public high schools, Westbury High and Overbrook, were scheduled on the same night as each other, but did not compete with the ones at the private schools, thus providing additional opportunities if one were desperate.

Fathers were particularly grateful for this arrangement as it controlled the outlay on dresses. Girls attending two proms would often shop for dresses together and swap for the second dance. It was not unknown for girls to make their own dresses in those days before proms became expensive extravaganzas.

As part of the special treat to herself after saying goodbye to her cousin Josie, Sally had splashed out on her dress for the Holly Ball. She'd put a deposit on it that day and collected it the next. Already, her mother had started the slight alterations it needed.

Sally had asked Tom Bradford before the Hayride and things had been going well until – well, until *things* pushed her into a meltdown. She could still not get over the way her friends seemingly fawned over her unsophisticated and socially gauche cousin, Josie; Patricia Detweiler continued to sail along serenely, as if unaware that her family's fortune had dwindled irretrievably. Then, during the Hayride, she had thought she'd seen ghosts in the woods – which had turned out to be Buzz Keogh and Stu Gardner messing around.

It had all proved too much.

Sally Hawes wasn't one to dwell on these failures of others, and after all, it had been a good week what with getting her life back with Josie's departure and picking up her dress.

☙

Saturday night would be the time to cement things. There was a party at Nick's. The group called them parties, but they were just a gathering of a flexible group of friends, not dress up parties. There'd be some food, mostly just nibbles, or, occasionally a pizza. People would bring their newest records – which ranged from the latest pop songs, albums of Broadway shows, jazz and even more serious music, if any of the more musical had been to a concert or recital. There might be dancing, but one could never be sure.

What there certainly would be is a lot of talking, either as one big group, or several smaller ones. Topics might include sports and holiday experiences or plans, what people were reading at school, had seen on television, politics, and debates on whether the local water should be fluoridated, and existentialism.

It wasn't a stupid crowd, and sometimes just about every one of them struggled to keep up or maintain an interest.

Buzz and Stu were usually the ones to break up the serious discussions by going into one of their silly routines or other antics, but in reality, both were very bright.

ℵ

John had been at Nick's for about twenty minutes before Patricia arrived. More than one person said that few people deserved to be attacked less than Patricia. The consensus was that Sally had some way to go before she was completely forgiven. Amy Armitage was close to Sally and did her best to defend her.

"We all act like idiots sometimes," she said. "It's not like Sally does it often."

"She was pretty mean to her cousin," John said, who had taken Josie on the Hayride. "When you know that something's only going to last a certain length of time, you put up with it."

John was about the only person who could contradict Amy as they'd been going out for over a year.

"Well, Amy puts up with you," Buzz cracked, before he could speak. "And there's no end in sight for her."

John and Amy looked uncertain, but everyone else laughed, and the tension was broken.

The door bell rang and Patricia came in. Nick greeted her with a big smile. He hadn't seen her since the Hayride, and he was happy she'd come and pleased to see that she walked into the crowd so confidently.

Her welcome was obviously over-compensated, but Nick stayed close and chatted to her easily.

Amy and John had moved to the corner where the record player was and were sitting on the floor sorting through 45s and albums. Once Patricia had picked up a drink, she joined them to see what was available.

Stu came by, munching potato chips. Buzz followed juggling a Coke and his crutch while trying not to bang his cast on the furniture. Buzz was the other casualty of the Hayride. While "playing ghost" in the woods, he had fallen into a hole and broken his leg.

He and Stu immediately started making comments about the music, and with some deft pushing, shoving and grabbing, the two of them managed to slip some American songs (if very old) into the stack of Beatles, Stones and Chad and Jeremy.

They were so funny about it, Patricia, Amy and John let them.

"Hey, did you hear who's actually going to the Holly Ball this year?" Stu asked, like at TV presenter. "The old Buzzard was asked by Laura Mason!"

The usually confident Buzz looked embarrassed and had the lights been any brighter, his redness would have resulted in five minutes of further teasing.

"There's no accounting for taste," John said. "I always liked her."

Amy nodded.

"She is pretty well liked," she agreed.

"I was really surprised when she asked me," Buzz said.

"We're all surprised *anyone* asked you," Stu said, and they laughed – Buzz with them.

"Seriously, though, I think she's a nice girl," he said, trying to act grown up about it. "I don't know her that well, but we've always got on."

"Are you going have that cast off before Christmas?" Patricia asked.

"If I'm not out of it by the time of the Holly Ball, Laura will kill me," he laughed. "Fortunately, they're supposed to take it off a week before the dance."

"She's a very practical girl at school," Patricia said. "Does well at things like art, crafts, and in labs."

"You've known her forever, haven't you?" Amy asked. "The thing is, she is only just social enough. She doesn't join cliques, but moves fairly well between the groups."

"That's good, isn't it?" John asked.

"I'm not sure," Amy said. "I never quite trust people like that. It might be why she invited Buzz."

"What might be?" Nick asked.

"Well, if you're on the edge of things, why not become associated with someone who is more – more the center of things, even if for being harebrained."

We laughed until Buzz protested.

"Hey! I'm standing here," Buzz exclaimed. "Well, more propped up, but I think she's a young lady of discerning taste."

"I rest my case," Amy said, and started to wander off.

Buzz and Stu had the wonderful knack of unifying people with laughter. While Nick, John and others had originally categorized them as goof-balls, over time, they had proved to be good friends – even though they were at Saint Benedict's, and Nick and John were at the Academy.

"Hey, is Sally coming tonight?" Stu asked.

"She wouldn't dare," John said, earning him a sharp look from Amy who replied:

"She wouldn't dare *not*."

John thought Patricia stiffened, but he may have been wrong.

When the door bell rang again and there were sounds of more people coming in, Patricia definitely stiffened.

"Well, will you look at that," said Buzz, gawping.

Heads turned, expecting to see Sally making an entrance as if the last two weeks had never happened, but it wasn't Sally.

"Tom Bradford with Claire Ricordi!" Buzz gasped.

The others stood up to see better.

Tom and Sally had been together on the Hayride and Sally had asked him to the Holly Ball, though after her meltdown, Tom told his friends he'd be breaking that date.

As of yet, he had not told Sally.

"This could get interesting," Nick said, joining Patricia after showing Claire and Tom the food and drinks.

"I didn't know they knew each other!" Amy exclaimed. clearly concerned for Sally.

Claire Ricordi – whose real name was Chiara – her fourth generation American family clung to traditions of the old country – had recently begun to be part of the school and party scene. Though everyone had known her for years, she had been in the background, both in looks and in participation at school.

The cause of her transformation had been her singing. She had always been in the school choir but only last year was selected to sing in a few duets. This led to singing some solos. For this year's big production, she was currently rehearsing the role of Katisha – for the moment – insecure enough not to let it affect her ego.

Perhaps it was that insecurity that led her to hang on to Tom the way she did.

Stu gave a low whistle.

"The Fourth of July might be early this year," he said.

John was the first to recover.

"Come on, Amy. We can't stand here staring at them. Let's say hello."

Though not keen on the idea, Amy let herself be led. Stu and Buzz went off in search of more food, while Nick and Patricia stayed behind.

"I don't think I could bear any more scenes," Patricia said, softly.

"Don't worry," Nick whispered in her ear. "You won't be involved in this one."

After one of Buzz's record selections dropped on the turntable, everyone laughed, but a few began to dance. While some dancing could happen at these get-togethers, it didn't always.

It was while listening, dancing to and laughing at the 1958 "Tequila" that Sally appeared. Nick's mother had answered the door and, knowing nothing about the Hayride episode (or at least not linking it to the girl in front of her), greeted her enthusiastically, and escorted her into the party.

Nick, who always watched his mother in case she did one of those things that mothers do that embarrass their children, had been paying more attention to her than to Sally. When he realized it was Sally, Nick stiffened, and after a second, left Patricia and went to greet her.

"Hi, Sally," he said, as neutrally as he could. "I think you know everyone here. There's some food here, and what would you like to drink?"

Nick poured the requested Sprite.

"Your mother's brownies?" she asked, eyeing the pile.

"Made this afternoon," Nick said.

"I might let myself have half of one later," she said.

Amy came up to talk to Sally, and Nick retreated back to Patricia, taking her a small sugar cookie. Patricia was watching as Nick's mother showed two more girls into the room.

Laura had been a friend of Patricia's since grammar school, and she had also known the other girl, Susan Jenson, since starting at Pinehill. Both joined them once they'd picked up a drink.

After initial greetings, Susan said:

"I can't believe how much work they're giving us! This party is going to be my last social event before Christmas!"

"No school, please!" said John.

"At least we have Thanksgiving coming up for a break," Patricia said, ignoring him.

"Break? More like catch up!" Laura exclaimed.

"I hear you and Buzz are doing the Holly Ball," Nick said.

Laura regarded him with suspicion, then replied.

"A girl's allowed a little fun once in a while," she laughed. "As long as Buzz doesn't make us the center of attention, it will be fine."

"And what you reckon the chances of that are?" Nick asked, but Laura saw he was teasing and laughed.

"I guess that's all of us fixed for the ball," John said. "It should be a great end to the semester."

As he spoke, and the others expressed agreement, the glimmer of an idea came to Patricia. Knowing what might happen later in the evening, a scheme was suddenly taking shape. She pushed it back as it was unlike most of her thoughts – but, perhaps, there was a way she could put it into action.

"Patricia?" Nick asked, and she realized he'd been talking to her.

"Sorry, Nick. I was thinking of something else. May I have another ginger ale?"

At such a small party, it was inevitable that Sally would see Tom and Claire quickly. They were sitting with a small group in an alcove of the L-shaped living room, partially obscured by the Christmas tree when Sally looked around the corner and saw them.

"Tom."

She said it in a voice of controlled authority, like the wife of a well-trained husband.

Tom looked around easily and smiled.

"Oh hello, Sally," he said. "There's a chair here if you like."

"Hi, Sally," said Clare brightly, not removing her arm from Tom's shoulder.

Sally stood there smoldering. If he took any pleasure in it, Tom didn't show it.

Sally didn't budge.

"I'd like to talk to you," she said, directly to Tom.

"Sure," he said, with the same friendliness, and indicated the chair.

"Alone," she stated. "In the kitchen."

Tom was about to offer resistance, but Claire took her hand from his shoulder and put it on his and told him to go ahead.

"Be nice to her," she whispered in his ear, smiling at him with a look for Sally to misinterpret.

As Tom followed Sally into the kitchen, three others quickly left.

ଔ

No one, except Amy, ever heard a first-hand account of the kitchen discussion but there was much speculation. Somehow Sally and Tom kept their "full and frank" exchange of views from being overheard. When Sally came out, Amy intercepted her, and they both left the party without saying goodbye.

All Tom would tell us was that he fulfilled his intention of telling Sally that as far as going to the Holly Ball with her was concerned, it was off.

Amy was a bit less discreet and it wasn't long before the boys from both Saint Benedict's and the Academy had heard her version.

According to Amy, Sally had demanded to know why Tom had arrived with Claire when everyone knew that she (Sally) was his girlfriend.

Tom had quietly replied that "everyone" knew no such thing. He went on to say, with a measure of control that poured kerosene on Sally's hot coals, that even she couldn't expect him to go out with her after slaughtering his friends.

"You really expected I would?" he had asked, shortly before she took a swing at him. She missed and didn't take a second swipe.

Tom had turned to go, but Sally couldn't control her fury and said in a gasping whisper:

"But I've bought a dress!"

According to Amy, this was what had upset Sally the most. Yet, it hadn't taken her long to express the view that boys were like buses: another would arrive before too long.

ꟸ

Indeed, she was proved right.

At the next party, the week after Thanksgiving, people had already heard that Sally had met someone new.

"I haven't seen him yet," Amy told Nick and John later in front of Dexter's Department Store while we were waiting for buses.

"He's new to the area. Graduated last year. Sally says, he's a *big* step up from Tom," she continued, relishing the gossip.

"And, he won't know any of her history," Nick said.

The boys laughed.

"I give it three weeks," John agreed.

"Over by Christmas," Nick said.

"I think you guys are mean," Amy said. "She's really very nice. She's an old friend; you should give her a break."

"So, are we going to get to meet this paragon, or is she keeping him under wraps until he's well and truly hooked?"

Amy considered her answer.

"I'm hoping to see them this weekend," she said. "I've not heard Sally so enthusiastic about anyone before."

Nick and John exchanged glances.

It was hard to credit Amy's statement as all Sally's friends had heard her enthuse about this guy or that, until he was downgraded to a subhuman level, eventually becoming a non-person.

Seeing their skeptical looks, Amy smiled.

"What choice do I have but to believe her? She's just about my best friend."

She turned and boarded her bus.

"And that should tell everyone something," John said.

☙

On the Monday before the Holly Ball, John and Nick bumped into Stu outside Dexter's. He walked up to them with a big smile and announced:

"He exists! Sally's Superman is real. I saw them at Friendly's having burgers and frappes!"

"Ah! A big spender!"

Though not really interested, it pleased John to get some information that did not come from Amy.

"Well?"

Stu knew he had an audience, at least until their bus came, which gave him fifteen minutes.

"Like you guys, I was doubtful that Sally could have found anyone so quickly," he began. "Given her present form, I'm guessing that she was going to dump Tom anyway, but he beat her to it."

"I'm not sure about that," John said. "Even I don't think she's that calculating."

"I have to say, David – or whatever his name is – is decent looking. Perfect Sally bait," Stu said, in his pseudo-flippant style.

Not being schoolgirls, Nick and John waited without comment for Stu to resume his narrative.

"They seemed to be having a good time, but things were reversed: Sally was acting soppy while David appeared to be detached."

"You mean he had several screws loose?" John asked.

"Don't start imitating my act," Stu said, with mock impatience.

"Sorry," John said, mirroring Stu's tone.

"The guy looked like an insurance salesman," Stu continued. "Clean cut, well dressed, good posture and manners.

"They chatted and smiled – Sally seemed to laugh at everything he said – and kept touching his arm or shoulder."

"She usually plays things much cooler," Nick said.

"I don't think your experience is anything to go by," Stu said, seriously enough for Nick to shoot him a sharp look. Then Stu burst out laughing. "Sorry. I guess all of us have been hung up on Sally at one time or another."

"Did you speak to them?" John asked.

"No. They were at the far end of the counter and I was collecting a takeaway," he replied. "She did catch my eye, and I waved casually, then looked at my wallet. I don't think she knew I'd seen as much as I did."

"The Holly Ball should prove interesting," John said.

"Is it going to be tricky going with Amy?" Stu asked.

"Not at all," John said. "She's fun and can't stop herself from talking about Sally and her friends. I keep telling her she shouldn't be afraid to be more independent, but she thinks I'm preparing her for being dumped."

"So, you might make it for the long haul to the Valentine Hop?" Stu asked.

"Let's see how well you and Laura survive Saturday," he retorted.

Before Stu could reply, he realized his bus had rolled up and lunged for his bookbag and a tennis racquet that he had with him for some reason.

☙

The best news from the Holly Ball was that Buzz Keogh had got his cast taken off before it. It wasn't back to full use, but Buzz didn't care because Laura was proving to be amazingly solicitous. She helped him in and out of the car (she declared that she would drive them), assisted him on the stairs, and made him rest between dances.

Buzz didn't need any of this, but wallowed in the attention. Stu wanted to call his bluff, but Nick and John stopped him.

"He's been in real pain – not to mention the hassle of being on crutches. Let him enjoy it," John said.

"Let them both enjoy it," Amy said.

Patricia and Amy laughed.

"Most boys are afraid we can't look after ourselves," she said. "We're physically tougher than we look. Emotionally – well, that's another story."

Nick and Patricia joined Laura and Buzz at one of the tables between dances.

"Laura looks amazing," Nick said quietly to Patricia as they approached.

"She does, it's because she's so obviously happy."

"Who would have thought that Buzz Keogh could produce such a reaction?" Nick asked.

Patricia laughed.

"Well, they're happy."

They sat down.

"How's the wounded warrior?" Nick asked.

Buzz laughed, and before he could reply, Laura spoke.

"He's making a brave effort," she said. "I don't want him to overdo it so we have to go home early."

"I'm not a geriatric," Buzz protested, lightheartedly. "I wish people wouldn't talk about me as though I weren't here!"

He then leaned over and spoke to Nick in a stage whisper.

"It's a great way to get attention and sympathy," he said. "Doesn't Laura look terrific?"

Nick agreed, while Patricia was talking to her about her dress.

"Who's responsible for this band?" Nick asked. "They're really good."

"That's the Senior Council," Laura said, turning to Nick. "Patricia's on it," she whispered, turning back to the table.

"A few of the girls had heard them before," Patricia explained. "Most of the band is from Westbury College."

"It's not often you see a mixed band," Buzz said.

"No, it isn't," Patricia agreed. "The girls are music majors. The one on drums is a senior, and the bass player is a junior. The guys are mostly seniors."

"Is it true they hate each other?" Laura asked.

"They've had their disagreements," Patricia admitted, but they can't argue with the success they've had."

"I wish they'd do something a bit slower," Buzz said. "I'd be able to do more."

"What you mean is you could hang on to Laura," Nick said.

"You know Pinehill," Laura said, "'Make them glow before dancing slow.'"

They all laughed.

"I heard they made the band change its name," Nick said.

Patricia and Laura laughed.

"The band is called 'Knockers,' for obvious reasons," Patricia explained, giggling. "However, playing here was something of a coup, so they agreed that for tonight they'd be known as 'The Knockers.' It's only marginally better, but it was enough for B.J. – uh oh, here we go."

Everyone looked towards the door as Tom and Claire came in.

"They're a handsome couple," Amy said. "She's looking very trendy for Westbury!"

Tom and Claire went over to a group of his friends to say hi before they began to dance.

Although the only decorations were two Christmas trees with clear lights and some wreaths, clever lighting made the room glow with warmth. Although dresses were dominantly red and green, there was a full range of other colors.

"Have you presented Nick to B.J. yet?" Laura asked.

B.J. Perkins was the formidable headmistress of Pinehill. Since this was a formal dance, the girls had to present their "guests" to her within an hour of arriving. While an old-fashioned formality, allowing some time for presentation meant that it avoided an even more formal reception line.

"No," Patricia said.

"Neither have I," Laura said.

"Let's go, then," Amy said, standing.

"Come along, Buzz," Laura said, helping him up. "You'd better behave or you'll go home in a wheelchair."

"A sedan chair would be better," Buzz replied, unfazed by Laura's shift from nurse to mother.

The others watched them walk slowly and carefully across the floor towards Miss Perkins. Buzz then suddenly stood up straight, executed a few perfect dance steps finishing with a twirl before going back to clinging to Laura and acting infirm.

"Watch him – he's going to pull something," John said, in a low voice.

"He wouldn't do that to Laura," Patricia said.

"It depends how confined he feels," John said.

Laura and Buzz were able to cross the dance floor more quickly than Patricia and Nick who had paused to watch their progress, and fell in line behind them.

The volume of "The Knockers" prevented them from hearing what was said, but Miss Perkins had been given a list of all the girls and their dates and somehow had memorized them.

No one spoke easily to B.J., so watching the normally confident Laura hesitate while presenting Buzz was not a big surprise. What was less expected was that when the redoubtable Miss Perkins extended her hand to Buzz, he bent forward and kissed it.

John and Nick burst out laughing but the girls looked horrified. But it wasn't over. When Buzz stepped back, he found that Miss Perkins had not let go of his hand. He looked down at it, and she pulled him to her, leaned forwards and whispered in his ear.

We were fearing it was a severe rebuke, but when Buzz looked up, he had a broad smile. Laura hustled him away as quickly as she could while we took our turns.

We danced for a while, said hello to other friends, and went into the anteroom where refreshments were served.

Laura was still berating Buzz. We thought it was for kissing Miss Perkins' hand, but it was because he had not told her what she had said.

"If you don't tell me right now, you can walk home!" she threatened.

"Calm down, Laura. I want everyone to hear this because I don't want to repeat it all night."

"Nice work, Buzz," Nick said. "How to make yourself memorable."

"And embarrass me nearly to tears," Laura exclaimed, with near fury.

They collected cups of punch (as yet unadulterated) and backed away from the crowd.

"All right. Enough! Let's hear it," Laura commanded. "What did she say to you."

Buzz stood to his full height and tried to put on a straight face.

"She said, 'Your father was a clown, too. Please remember me to him.'"

All three girls gaped while John, Nick and Buzz laughed loudly.

"Come on, let's dance," Buzz said. "I don't want to miss Sally's entrance with her mystery man."

Indeed, it was not long after they began dancing that Sally and David entered. She entered as though it was her private party, and she grandly toured the room saying hello to everyone and introducing David.

We actually stopped dancing to watch her introduce David to Miss Perkins. Her gestures were exaggerated, and even Amy remarked that she hadn't thought it possible to touch someone so much when introducing him to someone else.

David accepted the high school formality with aplomb, smiled graciously, exchanged a few words and led Sally to the dance floor.

"She's really gone, isn't she?" Laura shouted over the band.

Patricia was taking no pleasure in this and turned away and began dancing again. She was a minimalist dancer, but her moves were expressive. Sally and Amy were more flamboyant, while Laura was somewhere in between.

Buzz seemed to be holding up well and even Laura seemed to forget that he was supposed to be in recuperative mode. The music was good and dancing to a live band always added dynamism to a dance.

After about twenty minutes of gyrations, Buzz's stamina finally broke down. He wobbled and John grabbed him.

"It's only the damn leg," he shouted. "I'm not having heart failure."

Laura tried to help him back to the table, but he really needed John to support him. Amy took the opportunity to say hello to Sally and get a closer look at David. Patricia and Nick continued to dance, and the band shifted into a series of ballads. They danced a few of them before the band went back to full speed and volume, after which, they took a break.

Patricia went back to the table while Nick fetched some more drinks. Sally was just ahead of him in the line to the table.

"You haven't met David yet, have you?" she said easily, and introduced him.

They shook hands and exchanged greetings. He had a maturity unusual for someone just a few months out of high school, but he didn't look older. While one wouldn't call him wooden, his bearing was. Then it clicked. Nick felt pleased with himself and said nothing.

They chatted easily as the line inched forwards, but then Sally cut off mid-sentence and turned away from Nick, and David looked puzzled. Sally took him by the arm and turned him towards the food.

Nick wondered what he'd said to provoke this reaction, then turned to see Tom and Claire standing behind him.

"Tom. Claire. Enjoying the dance?"

"It's great," Claire said, enthusiastically. "Everyone looks so nice."

"They do, indeed," Tom agreed. "It's really crowded."

"Were you on the committee, Claire?" Nick asked.

"I didn't do much," she said.

"We were saying earlier how good the band is."

"They're actually playing stuff you can dance to," Tom said. "So many bands have no idea. They just want to show off and hope there's a record producer in the crowd."

"Several girls went to hear them at the college and at one of the schools in Fitchburg," Claire said.

"I hear there was a bit of a discussion about the name."

Claire looked embarrassed.

"I still don't like it," she said. "I'm surprised B.J. agreed so readily."

"She just didn't want her girls roaming all over the state checking out bands," Tom laughed.

Still looking embarrassed, Claire nodded. "You may be right."

"I don't know if you have a table, but when I left, there were some places at ours. In the corner near the emergency exit. Laura and Patricia are there."

Tom looked about to decline, but Claire beat him.

"That sounds great. Thanks."

Nick collected the drinks and headed back to the table.

"Tom and Claire might join us," he said, giving Patricia her drink. "Claire looked relieved to have somewhere to go that wouldn't involve Sally.

"Oh, and the hot food is just beginning to be served."

"Food!" exclaimed Buzz, starting to stand up.

"Sit!" Laura commanded, and everyone laughed, but Buzz sat.

"Tell me what you want," she said. "We'll bring it for you. I'm not risking you spilling food all over the dance floor, and I want to get a few more dances out of you before the evening's over."

Buzz made a face and shrugged.

"Don't worry, Laura," Nick said. "Buzz will eat anything. Shall I bring you some food, Patricia?"

"No, I'll come with you," she replied, then said to Buzz, "Tom and Claire will be here in a minute."

On the way across the dance floor, we passed the normally more reserved Sally practically climbing up David, who was doing his best to keep her at a distance to avoid attracting the attention of the roaming "Propriety Patrol" – teachers who had drawn the short straw and were delegated to ensure that there was room for a volley ball between the dancers during the slow numbers.

Patricia didn't stare but laughed.

The food comprised either meatballs or lasagna with French bread, a basic salad and small mince pies. While not a large selection, it was perfect for a winter's night and there was plenty of it. Only the use of worn cafeteria trays took the edge off what was a relatively stylish presentation.

Back at their table, Claire and Tom had set out their plates and put their trays against the back wall. There was recorded Christmas music playing softly in the background.

"Where's John and Amy?" Laura asked.

"Amy dragged John to talk to Sally," Buzz replied.

"This is nice," Patricia said, leaning against Nick in an unusual display of affection.

"Thank you for inviting me," Nick said.

Buzz had been watching them.

"No disasters so far," he said to Laura.

"Only because you've been kept on a tight rein," Laura said.

Tom and Claire had been watching their exchanges since sitting down, their heads going back and forth like watching a tennis match.

"These things are worth the risk," Claire said.

Tom turned to her.

"So, I'm a risk am I?" he demanding, feigning outrage.

"Better than a liability," Laura got in before Claire could say something that would dig her in deeper.

It was, of course, Buzz's laugher that united everyone.

"I don't supposed there's any chance of you getting me seconds?" he asked Laura.

She was ready to swat him until she caught the twitch in his cheek. She said nothing, but stood, took his plate and headed across the floor.

Tom whistled.

"I thought I was daring, but, boy do you like to live dangerously," he said.

"Sometimes, it's the person who is least obvious who is doing the most dangerous things," Patricia said, enigmatically.

When they finished eating (eventually, even Buzz), they sat back contentedly for a few minutes, watching the scene and talking to friends who dropped by. The consensus was that this was a better Ball than last year's, but no one was able to say quite why.

The band began playing again at eleven and played until midnight. In a nod to tradition, it had learned "Goodnight, Ladies," followed by B.J. taking the stage to thank everyone for their work, thank the band, and wish everyone a safe trip home and a Merry Christmas.

On the way out to the car, Patricia walked with her arm unashamedly around Nick. Once in the car, she said:

"I think I know why this was more special than last year."

Nick held his breath. While fond of Patricia, he wasn't in love with her and didn't want an awkward scene, and this was how they usually began.

He waited for her to speak, not starting the car.

"I think it's because it's the last," she said. "Who knows where we'll be next year? Wherever it is, it won't be here.

"It's been a wonderful evening, but bittersweet, too."

As usual, Patricia had been perceptive, cutting through sentimentality while still expressing sentiment.

His vanity did allow him to wonder why she hadn't fallen for him. Then again, she had invited him.

ഋ

In the various analyses of the evening, John and Nick heard numerous stories at the Academy on Monday, and Buzz and Stu shared a few more when they met at the bus stop in front of Dexter's.

"I've never seen anyone keep Buzz under control as successfully as Laura did," John said. "You would have loved it, Stu. Pity you weren't there."

"Buzz, sit!" Nick imitated.

"That gives me the chills," Buzz said.

"You loved it!"

"You're right, John. I had a great time," he admitted. "I paid for it all yesterday. I could barely move. I would have played dead this morning except I have a history test."

"What's the consensus on David?" Stu asked.

Nick and John looked at each other.

"Nice guy."

"Yeah."

"I barely saw him," John said, "but he was friendly enough. He did seem to have his hands full with Sally."

"She certainly had *her* hands full!" Buzz said.

They laughed.

Laura and Claire came around the corner and joined them. John filled them in on the conversation.

"It was fun," both girls said, casting affectionate looks at their dates.

"So, what's the word on Sally and David?" Nick asked.

The girls giggled.

"Oh, this is *it*! He's the one!" they laughed. "We shouldn't laugh, but we've never seen Sally-who-always-has-the-upper-hand-Hawes like this before, and we've known her since Kindergarten."

They laughed again.

"Right now, she's shopping for some amazing Christmas present for him."

"When is she seeing him again?" John asked.

"According to Amy, he's going to pick her up after school on Friday," Laura said.

"Where does he live?" Nick asked.

Claire and Laura laughed.

"That's part of why he's a man of mystery," Laura said. "*Sally doesn't know*. He picks her up and drops her off. He says he lives just north of Orange and Athol, but hasn't given her his address."

"What about a phone number?" Nick asked.

"No phone number. He calls her. Every day, but he won't talk for more than twenty minutes. He says her senior year is important," Laura said.

"And she's all right with that?" Stu asked, in disbelief. "What about her parents? Aren't they curious?"

"They've met him and, like the rest of us, think he's nice," Laura said. "He gave enough references to his house to satisfy them. They don't like Sally calling boys, so they like it that he hasn't given her his number."

Claire laughed.

"Sally says that sometimes when he telephones, her father answers and they talk about old cars for ten minutes," she said.

"She's furious with both of them because he takes that time off her twenty minutes."

"Does anyone know what he does?" Nick asked. "Is he at college?"

They all looked blank and shook their heads.

A bus rolled up and Claire, Laura and John picked up their book bags.

"Are you going to Henderson's party Saturday?"

They all said yes, and rushed off to the bus.

"I don't know about you, but I smell something fishy," Stu said.

"Confidentially, I had suspicions at the dance," Nick said. "I think he's a good guy, but he's not telling anyone much about himself."

"And you think you know why."

"Just a hunch," Nick said. "I don't want to be a jerk or mysterious, but – look, I'll tell you after Henderson's party. Maybe sooner."

"You'd better."

☙

Each year, the Henderson's gave a lavish Christmas party. Both Mr. and Mrs. Henderson had been to school with most of their parents. The Henderson's families were old Westbury industrialists, like the Detweilers, though they had enough money left to see them out. They had no children, so running out of money wasn't the problem that it was for Patricia.

It wasn't uncommon for there to be as many as eighty people at the party, though not all at once. People came and went during the evening, coming by before or after other events.

When their friends' children entered high school, the Hendersons included them in the invitation, and most put in an appearance. The food was good, there was a good possibility of sneaking a drink, and the Hendersons let them all use their tennis court during the summer.

Growing up, many of the neighborhood boys, like John, had cut their grass or shoveled their snow and been well-paid for it.

The Hendersons' was the one place, besides the Holly Ball, where it would be possible to find Tom

Bradford, Sally Hawes and Patricia Detweiler at the same place, and that held interesting possibilities.

☙

Six inches of snow was predicted for the night of the Hendersons' party, not enough to deter anyone from going.

The edges of the front walk and the long drive were lined with dozens of *luminaria* set into the snow and glowing. A peek inside the bag revealed that rather than small tea-lights or candle stubs, each bag held a thick candle about eight inches tall. They would probably burn until morning, if not later.

To look around the Hendersons' rooms, you would think they'd be overly protective and houseproud to the extent of paranoia. They had beautiful things, accumulated over several generations, and they were beautifully displayed. However, they weren't show pieces *per se*, but part of their home and lives. Objects to be admired, touched and used. Not many people would use an eighteenth century Ch'ing Dynasty palace bowl for serving ice cream, but as Mrs. Henderson noted, "Why not? It's the perfect shape. Anyway, this is a home, not a museum."

Why not, indeed.

The result was that teenagers who would normally have felt out of place, uncomfortable or bored, were happy to visit the Hendersons.

Nick and his parents arrived at the same time as John and his. They'd had to park down the street and walk through the new or fallen snow on the sidewalk or in the road. Most opted for the road lest the new snow hide patches of ice.

The front door was open but a heavy curtain hung between the vestibule, where there was a closet and several large chairs for coats, and the main hallway.

The house dated from the 1880s or 90s and had beautiful moldings, architraves and other woodwork. The hallway had large entrances to the dining room on one side and the living room on the other. There may once have been pocket doors, but none was visible. An elegant stairway extended towards the front door, dividing on a landing before doubling back to the second floor. Two small corridors ran next to the staircase to less used rooms.

Nick and John headed for the morning room, off the dining room, where the younger people gathered, but it was frequently invaded by parents, aunts and uncles who wanted to say hello. A number also took the opportunity to deliver Christmas presents, which mitigated the feeling of invasion.

Sally Hawes was there, talking to Amy. Sally apparently arrived just before John and Nick because she held a beautifully wrapped box that still carried the chill of the outdoors.

"Someone give you a present already?" John asked.

Sally twisted coyly.

"It's for David," Amy blurted, earning a peeved glance.

Sally thought a moment before deciding to brazen it out.

"He gave me mine Wednesday after school," she said.

"Does he know the Hendersons?" John asked.

"No. I asked if I could bring him," Sally said. "They said it was fine."

Nick was staring at the present.

"Have you opened it?" Nick asked. "I bet you couldn't resist a peek."

"No, I've been good. I haven't looked."

Amy laughed.

"But she's weighed it, shaken it, felt it so much that it's a wonder there's still ink on the paper," she said.

"I thought we could open ours together tonight, after the party," Sally said, not put off by the teasing.

"I think he looked like the wait until Christmas type," John said to Nick.

Nick nodded.

"That was my impression, too. He seemed pretty straight. Straight guys don't open presents before Christmas."

"No," John agreed.

The girls laughed at them as they moved on to see who else was there.

Tom Bradford was coming in with his parents as they crossed the hall.

"Good to see you," he said to them.

"No Claire tonight?"

"She's with a group singing carols at the hospital," he said. "She invited me, but if she heard my voice, I'd be out the door."

There was a table at the end of the sitting room where drinks were being served from an enormous punch bowl with an ornate silver ladle. Star-shaped ice cubes floated in the punch.

"Mrs. Henderson once told me it was an old wash bowl from the Bay State Hotel in Worcester," Nick said. "She's got the matching jug somewhere."

"As long as it doesn't taste soapy, I don't care where it came from," Tom said.

Nick felt a hand on his arm and turned.

"Hi, Nick."

"Good evening, Patricia. You're looking Christmassy."

We took our drinks to a relatively quiet corner, she wanted to go to the morning room, but I told her Sally was there waiting for Mr. Wonderful.

"She's got a long wait," Patricia said, softly.

Nick stepped back.

"Patricia?"

Her eyes glistened and he was afraid she was going to start crying.

"Nick, you and my other friends were so good to me after – after the Hayride," she began, struggling to control her voice and thoughts. "Everyone really did something to defend me, even Amy."

"That's because we like you. It's not like your grandmother was Lizzie Bordon – even that wouldn't matter, unless you suddenly developed an interest in splitting logs – I'm sorry, Patricia – "

She managed to laugh.

"You're sounding like Buzz," she said, smiling. "By the way, Laura's been walking on air all week. He was very good to her."

"She did all the fussing and work," Nick said.

Patricia sighed.

"Boys really don't see anything, do they?" she said, as if making the discovery.

"You're going to have to explain."

She sat on a small burgundy velvet loveseat. Nick joined her.

"He *let* her," she said, pausing between each word so he would understand. "He wasn't in that much pain – I'm not saying he was faking, but he didn't need *all* the attention Laura gave him.

"By letting her take control, he was showing his affection," she explained. "Don't you see?"

"That's how *girls* see it?" he asked.

"That's how it is," she said, firmly. "Anyway, I don't want to talk about Buzz and Laura."

"Did they have a better time at the Holly Ball than we did?" Nick asked, mischievously.

Patricia's reply was perfectly calm.

"No, they didn't. I'm walking on air, too, but that's not what I want to talk about."

Nick struggled to keep a straight face, sensing it was something serious. At least she wasn't cross with him, and didn't seem about to cry. Those were wins, weren't they?

"After the Hayride, my friends were wonderful. People like Amy, who were also close to Sally, had a hard time, but one by one, they checked up on me."

She paused.

"This is a confession and, Nick, I want you to promise that it goes no further. I need to trust someone now, and I think I can trust you."

The noise and laughter surrounding them was in sharp contrast to Patricia's present mood. The worst thing would be to be interrupted.

She smiled and took a drink, more to show she was having a good time and didn't need assistance from anyone.

"You can imagine that I was very hurt and bruised by what Sally said. At least, as her – her – *rant* went on, the target became more general, but there's no doubt that I – and my parents – were the main target."

She paused for another sip of punch.

"It's not a nice characteristic, but teenaged girls like to get even," she continued. "Revenge is too strong a word, but somehow, I wanted Sally to feel some emotional pain."

Nick was about to say something, but she touched his arm.

"I need to finish this, Nick.

"I thought hard. I needed to do something that had that effect but couldn't be traced back to me. It had to be something emotional, memorable and with no physical damage. It also had to be serious enough to make an impact."

Given the content of her speech, she didn't sound scheming, vindictive, or even mildly bitchy. She was just telling it how it was.

"I think I see where this is going," Nick said, with the flicker of a smile.

"You really mustn't tell. *Ever*. I'm not proud of it, but it's one of those things that has to be done – and I've been bursting to tell someone for weeks."

She took a deep breath.

"David is my cousin. He graduated last year and enlisted in the Army. He was probably going to get drafted, and he signed up to some program that would give him some training."

"Automotive training?" Nick asked.

Patricia looked up.

"Yes. How do you know?"

"Amy told us about how he'd call up Sally and talk to her father about cars, and how that drove her nuts," Nick said, with a smile.

"Yes. That's absolutely right."

"Let me guess: He's not coming tonight?"

"No."

"Where did he live while he was in Westbury?"

"With my family," she replied, noticeably relieved. "He was doing an East Coast tour saying goodbye to family before shipping out."

"Is he going to Vietnam?" Nick asked, anxiously.

"No. That was part of his enlistment package. He gets specialist training and a non-combat area assignment, unless things get really bad. He suspects he'll be going to Germany but it could be Nevada."

She was smiling now.

"Has he left already?"

"He's gone back home to Detroit. He'll start active duty after Christmas. He did his basic training in the summer, and finished his specialist training in November. So, he's had time to let his hair grow back."

Nick burst out laughing.

"And the present to Sally?"

"It's a beautiful scarf. I expect we'll all see a lot of it. Also in the box is a letter saying goodbye. He doesn't say where he's going or what he'll be doing. He will just be gone," she said, with romantic exaggeration.

Nick looked at her.

"You helped him write it."

She nodded.

"Don't ever let me get on the wrong side of *you*!"

"Open your mouth and you'll be there before you finish the sentence," she said, jokingly, but definitely not.

Nick moved on from that prospect.

"And what about David? Was he not under the spell of the wonderful Sally Hawes?"

Patricia laughed.

"He told me he had never met anyone less his type. He had a good enough time at the dance, but the rest of it he said was a real effort."

"She'll grow up."

"I know," Patricia said.

"When she does, you must tell her."

She nodded.

"I know that, too."

"Have you thought about when?"

Patricia thought for a minute.

"I thought at her bachelorette party."

A Place for Marcus?

A Place for Marcus?

As every married man knows, when you get married, you don't just marry the girl but also all her relatives and friends. Caitriona (Caitlin, or Cait depending on what phase in her life people met her; to me, she was Caitlin or Cait) had a superfluity of both: brothers, sisters, aunts, uncles, people she called "aunt" or "uncle," and myriad cousins. She also appeared never to have lost touch with anyone she'd been to school with, met on holiday or at a party. I know this, as many of them would show up. Sometimes without warning or known plans of when they'd leave.

Most people's friends had outgrown this behaviour before they hit thirty. Not Caitlin's friends – or family.

Some were outright freeloaders; others were very generous and would bring quantities of food and wine, and even cook splendid meals for us during their stay.

These friends ran the gamut from poverty to extreme wealth; from the devoutly religious to the agnostic and rabidly atheist. One was a Druid and another a Jedi. Social class had nothing to do with inclusion in Caitlin's fan club, either.

If London was cosmopolitan, so were Caitlin's friends.

What they all had in common was they were very clever in at least one field, and they were all incredibly well-read.

One of her friends, a dustman called Colin, had read virtually the entire library of Classical literature: poetry, drama and history. The difficulty I had was that he had no idea how any of the names were pronounced. While what Colin said was fascinating, it was difficult to discount "Aristo-fanes," "Ana-crion," "Semon-ides," or "Auto-lycus."

Many of these friends would pass through our lives every few years, while her closer friends would turn up every week or so, perhaps more often. These people lived in and around London and would only stay if the food and drink had been particularly good.

࿐

Caitlin is well able to cope with visitors, invited or not. She is tolerant, patient, and virtually unflappable. While I am always on hand to help her, menus and dishes appear with little visible effort. Five courses for six people with drinks and canapes? No problem, and by the time we'd sit down, she'd look as if she'd spent the previous two hours being pampered.

The only thing that genuinely seemed to annoy her was when people mispronounced "Caitriona" as anything except "Katrina."

Among Cait's best and oldest friends was Oona Whitney.

The daughter of an Oxford don (Classics) and a historical novelist mother, Oona undertook a wide range of temporary jobs. Eventually, this grew into short-term contract jobs at the upper end of middle management.

She had three conditions for work: nine-to-five hours (no overtime), an hour-and-a-half for lunch, and a contract of not more than four months.

"In your dreams!" I exclaimed, when Cait first told me this.

"She gets taken on every time, and almost always gets offered a permanent job at the end of her contract," I was assured.

"She must be good."

"She's *very* good," Cait said. "She doesn't take prisoners, but has no career ambitions. If she takes a full-time job, she loses her vacation time."

Oona took two, sometimes three, holidays each year. One for skiing, one on a ship or a beach, and a few weeks at a family cottage in the Cotswolds. Exceptionally, she would undertake a job that allowed remote working and would spend even more time in the Cotswolds.

Nice life.

If that weren't enough, she was also drop-dead gorgeous. Tall, slim, dark and feminine, she was hard not to notice in any social gathering. However, on the few times Cait and I had met her during a lunch break in town, she had managed to look ordinary to the extent of being barely noticeable.

Not long after I'd first met her (when my existence was barely acknowledged), I asked Cait if Oona had a boyfriend (or to be PC, girlfriend, or left or right transgender partner).

"She's got a boyfriend," Caitlin reassured me. "She's been with him for ages. Since college."

"What's he like?"

Cait shook her head.

"No idea. I've never met him."

I stared at her in disbelief.

"What?"

"No, it's true. I've never met him."

"But you're one of her best friends," I protested.

This anomaly didn't seem to bother Caitlin. She gave a slight shrug.

"She came to our wedding on her own?"

"Yes."

"Did you invite 'plus one'?"

"Of course," she replied, growing bored with the interrogation.

I couldn't resist asking, every time Oona was coming for a meal, "Should I set a place for Marcus?"

Over time, I managed to extract a few bits of information. Oona didn't really think Marcus was "presentable." Though they'd been together for nine years, he'd never met her parents. Indeed, he had never been mentioned to Oona's parents.

Later, Cait said she thought he was married.

"Not to Oona, I gather."

"No, to someone else."

"He just lives with Oona?"

"That's right."

"For *nine* years?"

"She seems happy with him."

While Caitlin was very tolerant, she was also very traditional herself. She respected and valued the social protocols of her parents, and while her friends might do things that she would never consider doing herself, she was never shocked. . . until. . . .

"Do you think he really exists?" I asked one Friday evening when Oona was expected the next day.

She would come for lunch, join us with other friends for dinner, and enjoy a leisurely Sunday with us.

We lived in a different part of London to her, so she enjoyed coming and walking through our neighbouring parks and woods.

She was easy enough company, but as I mentioned, I had not impressed her on first meeting. She had been one of our first guests after Caitlin and I were married. I knew about her parents, and, as I knew little about Classics, I had read her mother's book, *Daughter of Mauricia: The Early Years of Anne of Austria.*

I dropped that fact very subtly into the dinner conversation.

"Why would you waste your time on that?" was Oona's comment before turning back to talk to Cait.

This was why Cait was cautious about letting me talk too much to Oona. I reassured her that I'd never dream of asking Oona if Marcus actually existed.

"*Do* you think he really exists?" I pressed. "Or, is this some excuse not to have everyone try to fix her up with substandard men – like wearing a wedding ring when you're not married.

"For that matter, are you certain she even *likes* men?"

Caitlin stared at me.

"You've known Oona half your life!" I exclaimed, surprised by Caitlin's lack of curiosity "You've been to her flat, her parents, the Cotswold house. Where was Marcus? Under the bed? In the fruit cellar?"

Caitlin made no reply, but turned and walked quietly into another room and sat down.

I gave it five minutes then went to see her.

By then, she was moving some objects on a shelf and checking for dust.

"I'm sorry if I upset you," I said. "I just find it bizarre that in all those years, you've never met him."

She smiled at me and sat down.

"I was just shocked by the fact that I'd never considered it before," she said. "I always thought I was fairly perceptive, but, as you said, I've known her so long that I simply take what she says at face value."

"I'm – "

"No," she stopped me. "You are right: they are natural questions to ask. My problem is that – while I trust Oona completely – I want to find out more about Marcus now, too."

Caitlin was thinking and I didn't want to disturb her.

"It's going to take some time," she said, eventually. "I can't just give her a full-on cross-examination."

"There's no rush, unless he's coming tomorrow, too," I said. "Should I set a place for Marcus, just in case he comes?"

ꟸ

That particular weekend passed easily enough. I didn't seem to say anything Oona considered stupid, and Caitlin established that Marcus was in good health.

"Shall we just call Miss Marple?" I asked Cait on Sunday evening, after Oona had left.

"I'm sorry," she replied. "I ask questions all the time of everyone else, but just couldn't do it."

"Okay, how about making a list of what we want to know," I suggested. "Start with something simple. How long have they been together? Is he planning on divorcing his wife? What does he do?

"You might then suggest that you know her well enough that he could come one day."

"I can't do it all at once," she protested.

"No, of course not," I reassured her. "It's not that important, but by this time next year, let's see how many answers we have."

Rather than nag Caitlin for a year, when Oona's arrival for a meal was imminent, I continued to ask, "Should I set a place for Marcus?" It always got a laugh with the negative response.

Caitlin's efforts did not fail to yield the odd bit of fruit: Marcus and Oona marked their tenth year together during the year of our investigation. He worked for an insurance company in the City. He was eight years older than Oona.

Caitlin tried to leverage these facts into something traceable. During our year, Caitlin had the following exchanges:

"Ten years is a long time," she had said to Oona. "Are you going to celebrate?"

"He doesn't like celebrations," was Oona's reply.

"Maybe concert tickets?" Caitlin suggested.

"He's not a music fan."

"A weekend in the country?"

"He'd hate that. He really doesn't like going anywhere."

"Are you going to do anything for him?" Caitlin asked, in her final throw. "He's given you ten years of his life – and left his wife. Is he ever going to divorce her?"

"Our arrangement suits me fine."

And Caitlin got no more.

When we reviewed these few, useless facts, I could see that even she was becoming annoyed, if not suspicious.

"What kind of insurance does he sell?" I asked.

Cait just gave a long laugh.

"Oona would have no idea. She'd have no interest in what he does when he's not with her."

"Does he just live there? Does he contribute money for food, rates, utilities?"

"Oona can afford it."

"So, he's a kept man?"

I instantly felt I'd gone too far, but Cait just smiled.

"I suppose so," she said, with equanimity.

ᘓ

There was a major break-through during the summer when Caitlin had gone to spend the day with Oona.

Though she saw no sign of Marcus, she managed to catch a glimpse of an envelope on a table. It was addressed to Marcus Fowles.

"I saw it just long enough to get the name," she told me. "Then, Oona swept it up with her post and took it to somewhere in the kitchen."

She thought for a moment.

"What is it?"

Caitlin continued to puzzle something.

"Funny. The envelope was open, but with the pile of today's post – I recognised one of the catalogues that we got yesterday. And, the envelope looked – old."

"Old?"

"I saw it just long enough to read the name, but it was crumpled, not just in the way that it would be if it had been opened roughly, but as if it had been handled many times."

"You didn't see who it was from?"

"There was a blue logo in the corner," she said, uncertainly.

"Clever lady!" I exclaimed, embracing her. "That's something to work with."

At work, I had access to all the major business magazines from which I surreptitiously clipped every blue logo for insurance and financial services. My office was also near a large library and I was able to comb telephone and business directories. It was a slow process, but I began working backwards, in the event that Marcus had been sacked from his job years before and did nothing all day except wait for Oona to come home and cook him dinner.

When I'd amassed about forty logos, I put them in an envelope for Caitlin to look through.

She went through them all without any recognition.

"Sorry," she said. "It was two weeks ago now and I only saw it for a second."

She went off to do something, but I had an idea I wanted to try. I laid all the clippings out in rows on the dining room table and left them, and went off to start the charcoal grill.

About ten minutes later, there was a scream from inside, and Cait rushed into the garden holding one of the logos.

"It positively jumped out at me," she said, throwing her arms around me.

"I knew you could do it," I said. "What have you got?"

"Throgmorton General," she said, holding it up.

I had a name and a company. There was no guarantee that Marcus Fowles worked for Throgmorton, but it was a lead.

Oona would be meeting Caitlin on Saturday and then she'd come for supper and stay for Sunday lunch. That gave me Thursday and Friday to do some more research. I had to do it during lunch and after work, but once I had a name, picking up the trail was relatively simple.

The old, multi-volume London telephone books continued to be produced, albeit in limited numbers for institutional use, for far longer than most people think. There were other directories, too.

I picked up Marcus' trail at a date eight years before the time I write about, and two years after Oona took up with him.

Though I checked later references, I found nothing later. Moving backwards, I found the year when he had changed his address and made a guess that that was the year he'd got married.

On Saturday morning, while Caitlin and Oona were shopping, I spent some time on the General Register Office website. If the Marcus Fowles I found was Oona's – and the date of birth and marriage both suggested a high probability – he had married a Jessica Anne Langley.

I then tried to trace her and found a birth certificate and an address in Cheshire. Next, I had a look in the divorce index and found nothing.

Finally – and time was running out – just to ensure I had the right people, I checked the death records and did a general search.

It's often been said that it's a big mistake to Google your friends. It's a good principle. Perhaps it should be a law.

I found that Jessica Anne Fowles née Langley had died, shortly after Oona and Marcus had begun their arrangement.

Surely Oona knew this.

I then found an article recording her death in a car crash. "Fatal Crash on M25" was the headline. It had taken place on the then notorious section between the A3 and Heathrow where a large number of deaths had occurred, long before variable speed limits were introduced.

There was a picture of a lovely looking girl in her early twenties, and it was impossible not to feel a sense of loss. I took a screen shot and filed it with those of the various directory entries.

Why had Oona lied about this? Marcus was clear to marry her. Was she the one who refused? None of this was a reason to keep him out of sight, either.

I was about to shut down my laptop when I saw the article continued on another page. I clicked and then froze.

Also injured in the accident was Mrs Fowles husband, Marcus, 28. He was taken to Hillingdon Hospital where his condition is listed as critical. . . .

I heard a key in the door and Caitlin and Oona giggling as they entered.

"We're back, darling! Got the gin and tonics ready?" Cait called.

I took quick screen shots of both pages, filed them and shut down. Somehow, I'd have to put all this out of my mind for twenty-four hours and not let on to Caitlin that anything was amiss.

I left Caitlin and Oona pretty much alone over drinks as they discussed their shopping and mutual friends, but I was working in the kitchen and didn't have time to continue the research and find out what had happened to Marcus.

Presumably, he recovered. Maybe he had limited mobility or was badly scarred and therefore kept out of sight. It was possible, but didn't ring true.

Over supper, it was hard not to look at Oona and try to fathom what was going on, or what motivated her. While bursting to tell Caitlin what I'd found as we got ready for bed, I didn't want to give her an incomplete story.

I didn't get back to the computer until late Sunday afternoon. We had gone for a long walk through the woods with Oona, and then she stayed for tea. I kept trying to imagine what was going on in her beautiful head as she chatted easily about ordinary things.

After she had gone, and Caitlin and I had a chance to review the weekend and have a light supper, I stole away to my laptop. I found several more newspapers that had reported the crash and then scanned the issues for the next few days. (By this time, the searches were costing some money and getting me subscriptions to services that I knew I'd never use again. Such is the price of nosiness.)

About ten days after the crash, there was a poignant picture of a double funeral, naming Jessica and Marcus Fowles and pictures of the couple on their honeymoon in Funchal less than two years before. It gave no address or employment details, so there was still enough room for error that I couldn't yet tell Caitlin. Somehow, I would have to make the link between this Marcus and the one at Throgmorton General, but I had no idea how to do that.

☙

A few days later, the germ of an idea came to me, but it needed refining.

In the meantime, Oona had telephoned to thank Caitlin for the weekend. I answered the phone and, unusually, she took time to chat to me for a few minutes. She was talking about the differences between the book and the film of something all three of us had read. I was flattered that she finally seemed to think I was worth a conversation.

For an uncomfortable moment, I thought she was going to reveal that Caitlin had said something about Marcus to her, and she was going to warn me off. By this time, I was sufficiently disturbed never to mention his name again – but, she didn't, and after agreeing that one of the top earning Hollywood actresses had no idea how to act, and clearly didn't understand the roles she played, I handed over to Caitlin.

Towards the end of the week, I had refined my plan and during a quiet period at work, I picked up the telephone and called the personnel office of Throgmorton General.

"I'm on the board of a small charity, and I wanted to check on someone who works for you who is being considered as a trustee."

I named a tiny local woodland charity that was nearly totally dormant. This would explain the lack of current details on the Charity Commission site.

"The candidate is Marcus Fowles. According to his application he works for you. I also have a National Insurance number that you might confirm for me, please."

I gave a National Insurance number that was the same as mine except for two random digits.

"Since we're essentially restarting the charity, we really need people we can trust," I said in the silence.

I hoped I wasn't over-egging it.

"Of course," came the reassuring reply.

I heard the keyboard clicking, then a tiny intake of breath.

"I'm sorry to tell you that you may have to look for another candidate," she said. "The NI number doesn't match the one we have for Marcus Fowles, and according to our records, he hasn't worked here for a number of years.

"Our records say he's dead. I'm sorry."

"That's not good," I said, not expecting a comment. "Thank you very much for your help."

As far as I was concerned, that was it for Marcus. Eight years dead and buried. Now, all I had to do was tell Caitlin. What she'd do with that knowledge, I had no idea.

For once, we had a quiet Friday. Nothing to go to, and no one expected.

I waited until after we'd finished supper and were relaxing in the sitting room with the last of the wine.

"Caitlin, I really don't want to tell you this," I began, but – "

I looked up and saw her eyes had instantly filled with tears.

I looked at her quizzically.

"You're going to leave me," she whispered.

I moved quickly to her side on the sofa.

"No, darling! Never! Why would you even think that?"

"It was the way you were looking at Oona over the weekend," she managed to say. "I thought something was going on."

I tried not to laugh, as it was clearly the wrong thing to do, but I tried to give a gentle smile.

"No, darling," I said, totally taken off guard. "I was watching Oona because I was trying to work out what was going on in her head. Anyway, she's got Marcus – or maybe, she doesn't."

She looked at me, waiting for me to continue.

"I did some digging since you identified the logo," I started.

"Oh, that," she said, as if it were nothing of interest.

"I found Marcus."

That got her attention.

"He's dead. He and his wife died in a crash on the M25 – nine years ago."

Caitlin put her hand over her mouth and her eyes widened.

Suddenly she stood up.

"I've got to call Oona!" she said, heading to the telephone in the kitchen.

"*Wait!*" I cried, rushing after her.

"You can't do that!" I protested.

"I've got to tell her!" she declared, telephone in hand.

I put my finger on the plunger.

"Wait, Cait!" I said, too sharply and too loudly, but she stopped.

"*What* are you going to tell her?" I asked, now desperately trying to stop her. "Think of the consequences!"

Caitlin looked at me, patiently, as if I understood nothing.

"She's my oldest friend," she said, resolutely. "I've got to warn her that the man she's living with is an imposter!"

The Girl on the Train

The Girl on the Train Journal

Editor's Note

Encounters and adventures on trains have been a mainstay of fiction and films since passenger journeys began. Edgar Talmadge's short story, "The Girl on the Train," captures the piquancy and poignancy of such serendipitous encounters that we've all experienced when traveling, especially on trains. It combines a mundane encounter with a touch of fantasy and a dollop of *schmaltz*, so expertly slipped into the recipe that it has been swallowed before one's aware of it.

Edgar Talmadge (1919 - 2001) was one of those writers whose life was as well-known as his stories. As with many other such writers, there was a great contrast between the writing and the life. This is not uncommon; we find it in Hemingway, Fitzgerald, Lewis, Updike, Vidal and many others.

For those who knew Talmadge, the unsophisticated sensitivity of his characters and simplicity of his plots was always surprising. His own Baroque tastes and Byzantine involvements tried all of his acquaintance, his friends most of all. Jimmy Breslin said it better than anyone: "Talmadge can suffer in silence louder than anyone else."

Many a party or otherwise civilized social event was brought to a crashing end by one of Edgar's sublime sulks. It was refined to cause maximum effect with minimal effort. Norman Mailer put it (uncharacteristically) kindly when he said that Talmadge's writing had similar characteristics. Indeed, there was an effortlessness about it, though some was downright carelessness.

It was easier to like Edgar Talmadge's writing if you did not know the man, though Gore Vidal once remarked to know neither was better still.

William Faulkner appeared to subscribe to this precept. He never acknowledged Talmadge's existence. If asked about him, Faulkner would put on a blank expression and say, "Talmadge? Talmadge? Who's Talmadge?"

The fact remains that Talmadge made a good living from his writing and enjoyed a broad, popular following, and was well enough thought of to be included on undergraduate reading lists. His novels, *Above the Clouds* (1955), *Alizarin Tide* (1963) and *Honest Folk* (1967) have never been out of print. Yet, it is his first published collection of stories, *Out of the Orchard* (1956) that remains the favorite of his books, and one story, "The Girl on the Train," his most famous and best loved. Its heroine, Marianne Phalarope, has, improbably, entered the public consciousness as an incarnation of the indomitable spirit of youth.

The 1962 movie made from the story won five Oscars and was nominated for two more. It catapulted its young star, Samantha Wallace, into cinema legend, while the song that came from the film (an Oscar winner) is still played, regularly, in bars, restaurants and at dances around the world.

Edgar Talmadge guarded his literary output carefully. He claimed to write every day, but all anyone saw before his death were the four books he published. He wrote enough articles and reviews to ensure a basic level of comfort and gave only a handful of interviews, mostly in Hollywood. His last was after the publication *Alizarin Tide* in 1962.

Born in Hamilton, New Hampshire, he lived in the family home until he died.

While he traveled as a young writer, he always returned to Hamilton. Though he was contracted to be on the set of *The Girl on the Train,* he always maintained that he never saw the completed film, having gone to the men's room after the opening credits and eating popcorn in the lobby until it was over.

Talmadge kept to himself, grew vegetables in his garden and kept two horses that he occasionally rode in the woods.

His lack of output raised questions of whether he had gone dry. An old acquaintance and Talmadge's lawyer from Hamilton, Abner Goodrich, summed it up: "Edgar had as little to say in print as he had to say to his neighbors."

Talmadge, not unsurprisingly, never married, and though a millionaire many times over, his executors, when they disposed of his estate, said that it looked like all he'd bought in 80 years were light-bulbs and toilet paper.

Maurice Bonner, of A. J. Lattimer & Co., of Philadelphia, Talmadge's publisher and editor, had few personal dealings with his client, believing, in that wonderfully old-fashioned way, that knowing the writer would cloud the vision of the book. Bonner worked on all Talmadge's novels, though the short stories would somehow escape him, being sent direct to magazines.

If, after Talmadge's death, Bonner – Talmadge never had an agent (probably because he didn't want to share any more of his royalties than he had to) – expected to find a literary treasure trove, such as Edward Aswell, of Harper & Brothers, had found on the early death of Thomas Wolfe, he was sadly disappointed. Aswell had found a nine-foot tower of manuscript, from which he carved *The Web and the Rock, You Can't Go Home Again,* and several stories.

Bonner was known to have marked up a copy of one of Talmadge's stories in a magazine with edits and sent it to him. Talmadge shouted down the phone at Bonner for twenty minutes, but when the collected stories were published several years later, Talmadge had made all Bonner's changes.

Edgar Talmadge's farm yielded no such treasure. There were many books in the house, but as a collection, it was disappointing. The selection appeared to be only what the local dry goods store stocked: romances, thrillers, westerns, murder mysteries and other books of no distinction whatsoever. There was a complete Shakespeare, a Bible and a dictionary, but they proved to have belonged to his parents.

Shortly after his death, the editor of the *New England Review*, Quentin Delancey, had secured permission from Talmadge's executors (a retired local bank manager and his brother, whom Talmadge used to drink and play cards with) to visit the house to look for manuscripts or books that should be rescued.

Abner Goodrich, a dry Yankee, well past retirement age, handled the estate, and was probably the Talmadge lawyer because he lived nearer the Talmadge house than any other.

"Talmadge was an enigma, wasn't he?" Delancey had said.

"No," Goodrich replied. "He was like most people around here, just difficult."

That was all Goodrich said about him, too.

Delancey also found nothing. However, he made a name for himself for finding nothing. He wrote and lectured extensively about exploring the house, cellar and attic, and of talking to Talmadge's horses, now looked after by the farmer next door who hoped to keep them without paying for them. (Tourists happily paid to ride Talmadge's horses, even if they didn't know which ones in the stable they were.)

Delancey's best sentence from his lecture was, "The only publication in the house of the slightest interest was a 1910 Sears Roebuck catalog on the shelf in the disused two-holer."

Abner Goodrich eventually had an auctioneer come, and every last teacup was sold; then the horses, and finally, the house. The auction took three days, and since there wasn't a hotel within fifty miles of Hamilton, the merely curious gave up after the first day. The whole estate raised about $140,000. For someone with more than ten million in the bank, that wasn't a lot of property.

The truth is that most of the ten million came from the film of "The Girl on the Train." Talmadge had made a million on the movie in the first year or so, from the rights and the early royalties, but to everyone's surprise, the money kept coming. Then the sound track, television rights, re-releases, a growing number of merchandise deals, then video, DVD and all manner of advertising tie-ins. The "old Talmadge place" was bought by locals, a young couple, the Allens, as a weekend retreat from jobs in Boston, and eventually to retire there. [1]

Being locals, they did little to the house for several years, but when they eventually got around to tearing out the old kitchen counter, that had been coming away from the wall for about forty years, they were prepared to find decades of crumbs, desiccated rodents, and possibly some loose change. However, being New Hampshire, they didn't hold much hope for the last of these.

What they didn't expect to find was an old Woolworth's spiral-bound notebook, along with its 89-cent price sticker.

The notebook was nearly filled with closely written script in a variety of inks, indicating that it had been written over time. A few events referred to give clues to the period. Notably, there is a reference to "another damn broadcast" of *The Girl on the Train* on WMUR, a Manchester television station. Searches of the station records show that the film was broadcast seven times in the 1970s. There was one in September 1972 to mark the tenth year of the film's release, and then subsequent showings in 1976, 1977 and 1979.

---

[1] Of course, until the Allens bought it, the property had been known as the "old Peabody place," the Peabodys having sold it to the Talmadges in 1910.

That Talmadge didn't seem to have read much contemporary literature was further confirmed by his entries. Nothing written after 1960 is mentioned in the notebook.

While there are a number of anecdotes of his early life, and stories about the filming – which no one in Hollywood seems to have any recollection of (itself not a proof of fabrication, given the proclivity of film directors and stars to manufacture their own life stories) – there is nothing else to pin down the date of the composition.

One of the few things that gives a certain symmetry to Talmadge's rant, is the glimpse of his journey from Bangor to Hollywood to attend the filming. His diatribes against Samantha Wallace as Marianne are cruel, but Miss Wallace, now nearing seventy, shrugs them off. "It was worse in real life than it is in print."

Nonetheless, the comments are cruel enough.

Talmadge had no particular prejudice or phobia about flying. Jet services were well established between Boston and Los Angeles by 1964, and he flew across the Atlantic at least twice. It can only be supposed that he felt there was something fitting about taking the train to make that movie.

Perhaps he hoped he'd see another girl.

MR - June 2019

Characters & People

Marianne Phalarope - heroine of Edgar Talmadge's "The Girl on the Train"

Nicholas Dupris - the man on the train

Samantha Wallace - actress who played Marianne Phalarope in the film version and won an Academy Award

Norma Richards - the actress Talmadge wanted to play Marianne

Claude Bertani - French actor who played Nicholas Dupris

Curtis Kavanagh - screenwriter of *The Girl on the Train*

Martin Baldwin - director of the film *The Girl on the Train*

Aram Grigoryan - producer of *The Girl on the Train*

Maurice Bonner - Talmadge's editor at A. J. Lattimer & Co.

Alternative Story Title: "The Girl on Platform C"

Alternative Film Title: "*Changing Trains*"

"The Girl on the Train" Journal

By Edgar Talmadge

The breath-taking instant, not capturable, not repeatable, but universally recognized, at least by men of a certain age: a glance of unexpected beauty, human or natural; sometimes nearly caught on film – a wide-eyed look, a flash of color in a bird's wing, or an unexpected view – but the 'instant' that the Romantics glimpsed and wrote about.

That's what I had seen in the girl on the train who became Marianne. From the *augenblick*, to a detailed surreptitious study, to the emergence of a slight story, then the film, then the musical, then the iconography that collides with the crass merchandizing of *that face* on T-shirts and mock-Warhol posters.

Samantha Wallace says that the film role of Marianne Phalarope ruined her career because she could never get parts beyond that character, but the truth is, she ruined the film and the story for me and came close to changing my memory of a magical moment.

It is only with effort that I can recreate the original image in my mind, in the dark quiet of the night, and then, of course, not really satisfactorily.

A rummage through the libraries returned fewer references to the phrase "the girl on the train" than I had expected. I had thought it a trite title that had been in use since the days of Stephenson, and suspected that P.G. Wodehouse had written at least three stories of that name. He seems not to have done even one, though a character in *Love Among the Chickens* is said to have fallen in love with a girl on a train once.

Inevitably, the search turned up more references for the film, musical and song than it did for the original story, along with a nauseating volume of references and pictures of the – good word needed here - I just used nauseating; loathsome? Wretched? No one appreciates the former power of that word. Excremental? Insignificant. Closer. Inept? Inconsequential! Yes, the inconsequential Miss Samantha Wallace.

Oh, *why* couldn't they have let you play the part, Norma?

ꕥ

I was never a starving writer, which may have been one of my problems, but as so many of my generation, I found myself in Paris, writing, teaching a little English, and calling home for more money. It was only a middle-class spoiling. I wasn't extravagant, or even colorful in those days.

I wrote anything I could, proof-read the English on menus in return for a meal now and then, and acted as an unpaid tourist guide for a succession of family, friends and those they referred to my services.

I was going to stay for two years, but it turned into nearly three. Once my French was good enough to argue with people, there was no rush to get back to – where? That was the other issue. I knew my best chance was to complete the cliché and go to New York. I'd rather have gone to San Francisco or Boston, but the magazines and publishers I'd need to bother weren't there.

I tried to travel around France while I had the chance, and the trains were cheap enough, and it was possible to sleep on them, so I explored cities and towns, large and small, and tried to pick up one idea from each trip: a scene, a character, a bit of dialogue, or just a phrase.

I have a notebook of words and phrases that I thought would be useful one day. It's as near a !writer's notebook" that I ever got, but there's hardly anything coherent in it; just a collection of two and three word combinations, and a few lines of pointless dialogue. *The Great American Novel* might be in there, but I haven't found it yet. [2]

ᴕ

According to Charlton Heston in *The Agony and the Ecstasy*, Michelangelo used to see his figures in the blocks of marble, and then he only had to liberate them. I wish it were that easy in literature. You wrack your brain for a good, original plot, and someone comes along and writes something that's so unbelievably simple, honest and readable that it makes you want to spit. The only consolation is that Harper Lee never wrote another novel. [3]

I didn't mind that as much as successful *merde*, like *Peyton Place*, that I could have written had I thought it worth the time, but that would have ended my "promising" reputation. The public goes nuts for rubbish at one end of the spectrum, while the critics love the incomprehensible. The women are the hardest to take. I

---

[2] This notebook was never found.

[3] Talmadge died before the publication of *Go Set a Watchman* in 2015.

can't read Joyce Carol Oates, for example. Flannery is okay, but at the end of her stories I always think, who cares?

There are little gems of short stories, though. Flannery's "A Good Man is Hard to Find" is as devastating as Shirley's "The Lottery" or Katherine's, "The Fly." Tight, pithy stories that chill you to the marrow. Hawthorne was good at it, but so few writers have the necessary discipline.

The trouble is, they're short story writers who write novels. Scott and Ernest never should have written anything over fifty pages. Below that length, they were masters. In England, Willie Maugham did it as well as anyone this century, but the very great novels just aren't here.

Sometimes I think it's because it's all taken too seriously. Back in the days of Moll, Tom, Tristram, Pamela and the others, these things were fun. Dear old Jane could do it, too. Few have matched her eye and ear for observation. Her characters don't sound like each other – there's enough to them to imagine them as real. It's wonderful to get irritated with Emma, Mrs. Elton, or the unspeakable Thorpe siblings.

The Brontë dears managed it, too, but since then – Thackeray, Scott, Cooper, Dickens, Twain, James, Trollope, Galsworthy and the rest – no one's known when to stop.

The success of the 18th Century novelists, and Jane Austen and the Brontës is that they really had no idea what they were doing. They were just writing what they wanted to, with little hope, or even desire for publication, let alone recognition and immortality.

Striving is a terrible thing. When you shout, "Notice me!", there's a terrible risk that people will.

Who has written good novels? Something I'd never say in public in a million years.

Noel Coward wrote, "extraordinary how potent cheap music is." The same can be said of fiction, for of all the reading I've done, it's the "popular novels" I've loved more than the classics. The ones above go without saying. *Mockingbird*, too. Novels don't get better than that. But the others?

The Caine Mutiny. Rebecca. The Last Convertible. The Magus. Lolita. They may not last, but they certainly said something to their time. They had strong characters; good plots; readable prose. That's a novel.

There were a few shining more literary books: *Brideshead Revisited. Brave New World*. Ellison's *The Invisible Man. The Rector of Justin.* Louis can write. I'm not sure how much he has to say, but *Rector* was very good. At least they never tried to turn it into a film. People always want to talk about Gore, which is fine, as long as you don't have to talk *to* Gore, or worse, *listen* to him. But *Burr* and *1876* were great books. Great novels.

I hate to admit it, but *The Rise of Silas Lapham* and *The Turmoil* are two books I reread regularly. I first read them in my sophomore year at Exeter and, I suppose, they were my first real engagement with literature. Howells is underrated, but too steeped in his time for much to be revived besides *Lapham* and an acknowledgement of *Altruria* as a notable contribution to utopian literature. For the serious reader looking for a lost gem, his *A Hazard of New Fortunes* will well repay the reader.

As for Tarkington, well, film students will be led to *The Magnificent Ambersons*, but *The Turmoil* continues to reward, with its parody of Dickens, and clear exposition of the rhythm of American social change. Now, *that* would have made a good film.

The *Age of Innocence* is very fine, too, and even *Babbitt* and *Dodsworth* are worth a reconsideration, but they are historical pieces now, not living literature.

Popular fiction is about Money, Sex and Death.

Literature is about God, Love and Death.

Today, it's as difficult for most people to distinguish between God and Money, and Sex and Love as it is to distinguish between popular fiction and literature.

I asked for love, you gave me sex.

I wanted understanding, and you gave me psychoanalysis.

You see? It's just like the novel. When you try too hard, or think about it too much, greatness slips through your fingers.

Death, people just don't bother to think about. We're not used to it. It's not a part of our daily lives. It happens somewhere else. People who lost their mates and six children in one year knew death. It was an experience they shared with more than half the population.

So, filled with my own, wonderful ego, where does that leave me? I must write literature because there's not enough money, and a dearth of sex. God help me.

ꕥ

May 14, 1961
Logan Airport

Why isn't flying as elegant as taking a train? Is it the fear of meeting a sudden stop, a fiery death or a chilly, high altitude plummet? Or is it that the whole pre-travel experience is so regimented and restrictive?

No doubt, one day, people will look back at this period of air travel and think it the height of luxury, convenience, comfort and all the things it's not.

It's hours to Los Angeles. If I traveled by train, it would take days, but the views and the company would be far nicer.

ೞ

South Station

Called Howard to tell him that I'd be coming by train and I'd see him in a few days. Well, I told his secretary. She didn't sound happy. Said something about a press event tomorrow.

Easy change of plans. Taxi from Logan to South Station. I've got a bedroom on the *New England States* (joining the *Twentieth Century Limited* in Albany) and rolling into Chicago tomorrow afternoon. Then, the *City of Los Angeles* to California. (The ticket clerk recommended the *Super Chief*, but I don't like the Santa Fe's attitude.)

The bedroom is comfortable, my window is clean and there's plenty of space to read and write, good food just down the corridor and a comfortable bed. Who knows who I might meet in the dining car?

The fish was quite good, and the white wine even better, but the company was dire. Fortunately, I was seated by the window facing south and west, and had the most splendid view of the evening light on the landscape.

The couple seated opposite made a desultory attempt at talking to me until they apparently decided I was as dull as they were and gave up conversation altogether, speaking only to the waiter.

Back in my compartment, I read and wrote until the porter came to make up the bed, then I read until I nodded off.

It's curious, but you wake at different times during the night convinced that the train is racing out of control, or going in a different direction than it was when you went to sleep. Of course, in France, the latter is likely to be happening. Quite substantial towns on the route of night trains were ones that had initially resisted the railways and only later demanded a station. These were often, by necessity, termini that required to-ing and fro-ing to get in and out of.

Nevertheless, sleeping in a berth on a train is one of the great pleasures of life, if you can get the temperature right.

&

May 15th

Not running too late. Time for a leisurely lunch, a nice open steak sandwich, before gliding into Chicago for the real fun of the *City of Los Angeles*. [Note to any future readers: I am speaking ironically. For all their luxury, views, good food and the cruise-length journeys: the western trains simply never had the cachet of the East Coast trains, the *Shasta Daylight* came close.]

I pick this narrative up in the Palmer House. *The City of Los Angeles* leaves early afternoon tomorrow. Why people could never cross the country on a single train is one of the mysteries of the world.

Imagine archeologists digging through the ruins and trying to make sense of the transcontinental American Empire and wondering why it wasn't possible to go from Boston, New York or Philadelphia to San Francisco or Los Angeles without a layover in Chicago or St. Louis. They'll make up wonderful theories relating to rituals that needed to be carried out on the shores of Lake Michigan or the Mississippi, or ideas about our attitudes to the healthiness of staying on a train that long. It will never for a moment occur to them that it was because four of the greatest corporations the world had ever seen – blessed with engineering and commercial geniuses – simply couldn't get their acts together sufficiently to make it happen.

I guess that's why Chicago has so many good hotels.

ꟹ

The room on *The City of Los Angeles* is pretty good. Not *the Twentieth Century/New England States*, but not bad. There's something of a western theme playing with the geometry of the patterns and the colors. The first twenty-four hours is just cornfields, and it is best that most of it is crossed at night. The flatness means that the speed of the train is more constant, and there isn't the feeling of the engines laboring up long gradients. It makes for a peaceful night with only a few stops.

Apart from the literary short stories that I am seen with in public, in the dining car, or observation car, I am reading Agatha Christie. I always read Agatha Christie when I travel. I have done so since my high school days. There's nothing like a reassuring murder when one's away from home.

I always wanted to write a murder mystery. I can't, though; I'm a literary writer. If I suddenly published *Death on the Twentieth Century Limited,* the critics would eat me alive. I have thought about writing it under another name, but it would be impossible to keep a secret. I couldn't disguise my style, and it would be recognized sooner or later. These things always get out.

I've got the germ of a plot that involves a sedate college campus, academic rivalry, undergraduate intrigue, corruption in the athletic department and manipulation of the scholarships. There would be some mathematical element to the murders that would throw suspicion one way, while the real culprit was a philosopher or sociologist.

I read too late into the night, enjoying the speed and rhythm of the train. It was after two when I turned out the light. The result was that I slept until after ten, missed breakfast and had to bribe a porter to organize bacon, eggs, toast and coffee, which I must say he did cheerfully. Ten bucks didn't hurt, either.

I went for a late lunch and had a few glasses of red wine with an acceptable Welsh rabbit, a satisfying simple meal, like a *croque monsieur* that is all too often made badly. No one interesting was in the dining car. A woman, who must have been similar to Molly Brown, was holding forth at a table further down the car. Though colorful and opinionated, she's unlikely to have the same opportunity of immortality as Mrs. Brown. Thank heaven for small mercies.

I managed to write for three hours after lunch, then washed up and treated myself to a few Tom Collinses in the bar of the dome car. We're rising out of the desert now, but so close to the mountains on the western side that it was nearly dark before dinner was finished.

There was some congenial company in the dome after dinner, and we bought each other several rounds of drinks and talked until after eleven. Typically, on a train to Los Angeles, everyone talks about himself and hasn't the least interest in anyone else. In this way, I was able to remain *incognito* and assume the role of the little man who was impressed with the future success of everyone else. Inevitably, there was a youngish lady who was destined to be an actress – she'd fulfill the part of one of the corpses in my murder story nicely – and a very young man who was determined to be a screenwriter. Others were equally ambitious, but more parasitical: a real estate developer, a banker, and a quiet fellow who wanted to design costumes. I held no hope of success for any of them apart from the quiet man who seemed to have more about him than the others – the chief thing was that he wasn't impressed with any of them. He could go far.

☙

May 25th

The trouble with journals is one feels a moral obligation to write in them every day, and that's not my style. I don't mind writing every day, always have, but making notes, writing prose and doing real work is different to journal-keeping.

The City of Los Angeles delivered me to my destination six hours late, which suited me fine. The reporter and photographer sent to record my arrival had left by then, as had the studio big-wigs so that the only people left were a script girl called Ellen and her boyfriend, John, who was an assistant in the studio's PR department. Their combined age was less than mine, and they were nice enough kids, once they relaxed a little.

The studio had booked me a suite at the Ambassador Hotel, but I had booked simpler accommodation at the Biltmore. They were supposed to take me to some cocktail party, but it must have been over by the time the train arrived, so I got the Red Cap to take my suitcases to a taxi and we all got in and went to the Biltmore.

"When I get on the set, everyone is going to think I'm a cranky old man," I said. "I am with strangers and people who don't know what they're doing. You two had the patience to wait for me, even though you didn't want to, and you've been pretty nice. Now, John can write his press release, and you can have a drink, while I have a shower."

I had a trolley of liquor sent up to the room and disappeared after pouring Ellen and John some well-deserved drinks.

When I had changed, I poured John and Ellen another drink and let John interview me. He asked the usual studio bullshit questions, but then asked some of his own, which were interesting. On the strength of that, I called downstairs and booked a table for three for dinner.

"You were supposed to have dinner with Mr. Grigoryan and Mr. Kavanagh tonight," John said nervously.

"Fine," I said. "Where are they?"

"They were at the Ambassador," Ellen said.

"Did you call them and say I was here?"

"Yes, sir," said John. "I spoke to Mr. Baldwin's secretary."

"And he didn't call back, or say he was coming over?"

"No, sir."

"I think he blew his chance for dinner with me, then." [4]

Ellen and John laughed nervously.

I had a nice meal with them, and we stayed friends during the whole production. It was fun turning down invitations from Samantha Wallace, Claude Bertani, Aram Grigoryan and others and then meeting Ellen and John in an ordinary eatery for a working man's meal.

Once Samantha Wallace was cast as Marianne Phalarope, I had no loyalty to the movie. It was a liberating idea. I had my money; I didn't have to do anything, but having me on the set would be good publicity, and good publicity meant that more people would see the film and the more royalties I'd get. I didn't have to do anything apart from not bringing the film or studio into disrepute and I would have been a rank amateur at that.

That meant that I could be in Hollywood on my own terms. I didn't have to do a goddam thing I didn't want to.

---

[4] A scribbled note in the margin reads: "Both Grigoryan and Kavanagh tried to have dinner with me several times during the shooting, but I

told them they'd blown their chance. It was fun watching them try to get me to agree, and they tried all sorts of bait, but screw them."

ଔ

May 26th

Filming had, in fact, started before I arrived. That was the price of taking the train – I missed three days of additional agony. They had shot a few unimportant scenes from the middle of the story, mostly just to get something in the can quickly, and to let Claude and Samantha get used to working together.

The plot of "The Girl on the Train" is a very simple one. It's set in France in the late 1950s – the time is unimportant. It's a long-distance train to the south, exactly where is also unimportant. A girl in her early twenties has just broken up with her boyfriend in Paris and is heading back home to Clermont, or Poitiers or Limoges to an unexciting future without love.

She is humiliated, angry, and alternately defeated and defiant. She's in the restaurant car pushing her food around her plate in a frustrated fashion when she is joined by a man her father's age. They talk and the result is that to save her from going back and having to admit defeat, she can live with him. He's a widower with a large house on the outskirts of a mid-sized town and grows grapes, or flowers, or something.

She lives with him in an ambiguous relationship, regains her confidence, meets an agreeable young man and leaves the man on the train. In the last chapter, the older man sees her and her young man off on a train, and then gets on one heading the opposite direction.

It was one of half-a-dozen stories I published in a collection in 1956. I've written better things since, but there are some stories that resonate at a particular time and I was lucky enough to have this one become very popular.

There was no particular reason that it took five years to turn it into a movie, but Hollywood has its own peculiar pace. It's as though the wild private lives of those in the business are only frenetic because their day jobs are so excruciatingly tedious.

Having watched the film being made, I would rather have a job as a clerk in a very large insurance or accounting firm than have to do that every day. It's indescribably grim, and the sad fact is, most of the films produced are grim, too.

☙

9 June

Words cannot describe how far from Marianne Phalarope is Samantha Wallace. Marianne was well described in the book as being quite tall – five ten or so – dark, slight to the point of being skinny, and not possessed of the sort of looks that turned heads.

No man would ever dump Samantha Wallace, so the premise of the film was implausible from the start. Of only average height, Samantha's curvaceous body wasn't close to the stick-insect of the original. A blonde whom anyone would notice within a millisecond of entering the same room, Samantha Wallace was simply wrong for the part, and I could not acknowledge her as Marianne Phalarope.

We were introduced on my first day on the set. She smiled sweetly enough, but I wasn't impressed. I sat in my director's high-chair with "Mr. Talmadge" printed on the back and watched the proceedings, occasionally making a note in the copy of the script I had been given, but my notes were for this journal, as I had no input to the film. I was there as a courtesy and as a publicity tool.

I told everyone they were doing "marvelously" and praised every day's shooting. Had I said I hated everything would have made no difference and could have provided grounds to try to cut my fabulous salary.

I gave all the interviews the studio told me to and was very pleasant, kindly and bland to everyone. The sad fact was that no one ever asked me an intelligent question. Did I like Hollywood? What did I think about the way films were made; weren't Claude and Samantha wonderful together? Did I think they were having an affair? No one thought to ask if I was actually doing anything, or if I were bored senseless.

ฆ

19 June

Martin Baldwin, the director, isn't a bad guy. He does things efficiently, seems to have a good relationship with the cast and crew, and is smart enough not to over-rehearse scenes before shooting them.

I understand that it's not uncommon to shoot the same scene thirty times. I don't think he's done more than a handful more than six. It makes me wonder how it's all going to turn out, but when we view the rushes, he seems happy enough. We're at least a day ahead of schedule, which is admirable, and no one complains about being over worked.

He starts rehearsing at eight each morning, and wraps up at five, with only a few short breaks, and strictly one hour for lunch. He can't be more than thirty-two, but he's well-prepared each day, knows all the lines by memory – which is a fantastic asset when directing – and he lets his crew do what they need to. He doesn't argue with the camera man, the sound man, or anyone.

He seldom looks through the view-finder, but his eye for detail is excellent.

"There are supposed to be four glasses on the table. There are only three."

Even then, he doesn't shout at the props man, rather he thanks him warmly when the missing glass is set in place.

I invite him to dinner at the weekend. He demurs, saying he wants to spend time with his family. I ask if there's a place that all of them might like to go to eat. He suggests a restaurant near the beach at Malibu, and I agree to meet them there.

His wife, Alice, and children, Chip and Sally, are as pleasant as he is. He has chosen a restaurant on the beach so the children can go off and play in the sand while we talk. Alice is down to earth, a mid-western farm girl who feels out of things, but doesn't want to be in them.

"Martin has a job to do and he does it. I think he does it well," she said.

She's prettier than she knows, and is genuinely unspoiled.

"One day, he'll have a big success and things might become harder, but for now, it's not a bad life."

How often does one meet somebody who actually believes Oscar Wilde's aphorism, "When the gods wish to punish us, they answer our prayers"? Alice certainly did.

Chip and Sally were well-behaved, though eager to return to the beach, and made intelligent contributions to the conversation. Sally, who was about eleven, carefully explained to me how the Pacific Ocean worked, and was curious about the Atlantic, which she understood was not nearly as friendly.

It was not until we had finished our meal and Alice had gone down to the water's edge with the children that Martin asked me, point-blank, what I thought of the film.

I told him how I admired how he ran the production, and all the things written above, but he pressed me.

"Do you like the film so far?"

I looked out to sea, then took a long puff on my cigar.

"I wanted Norma Richards to play Marianne."

Martin looked down. He was clearly disappointed at my reply, but gave it some thought.

Then he looked up and directly into my eyes.

"That's about as different from Samantha Wallace as you can get," he said.

I stared back, then laughed.

"It sure as hell is."

He laughed, too.

There was a moment's pause, then Martin asked:

"Is it true that you still drive a 1932 Packard?"

"It's a 1930."

"Even better!" he smiled.

We never spoke about the film again.

☙

27th June

I notice that I have put 'th' or 'nd' or 'st' after some of the numbers in this journal. I must be bored. It's the mark of someone who doesn't want to get on with the writing. I never do it usually. My fourth grade teacher told us that it was not a proper thing to do, and I almost never do it. If this gets published, I hope I remember to edit it out.

Well, today was pretty strange.

I haven't been sleeping all that well. The Biltmore is a great hotel and I'm enjoying being here very much. It's comfortable, friendly, private and not too obvious about its pretension. The food is good, too, and no one seems to mind bringing me bowls of GrapeNuts at odd times.

The sleep business comes from the odd hours that people in the "industry" keep. Those who are working are up at four-thirty or five to be on the set by seven, and are tucked up by about eight-thirty. Those who go to parties are the ones who are "resting" – the quaint word for being out of work. They party hard because they need to be noticed again.

What a bowl of neuroses Hollywood is. People are miserable when they're working, because it is very hard work. There are dozens of people waiting for you to get some little thing, like lighting a match or tying a shoe, just right and they'll film it ten times just so they have some choices later on. They also spend a fortune filming scenes they know they'll never use. You can't tell where you are as everything is out of order.

All these things have made the last few weeks the most boring of my life. I'm not doing anything either, as I have said before. Martin asks me after each shot he thinks is good if it's okay with me. I agree, and he seems very pleased.

Well, today, Samantha Wallace spoke to me for the first time since we started. It was the first of two encounters.

During the lunch break, I stayed in my high-chair, in the shade of the set, writing a new short story. It's going all right, and I can write in most places. Noise and interruptions don't usually bother me, so I'm not grumpy about being disturbed. At least not too grumpy.

Samantha returned to the set early. She walked through the artificial street, familiarizing herself with the location of the lamp-posts, vehicles, curbstone, doorways, and so on. She had nodded to me when she got near enough, but was intent on working out her comfortableness with the set.

I continued to write until, after a few minutes, she approached me. When she spoke, she wasn't aggressive or timid.

"Why don't you like me, Mr. Talmadge?" she asked.

I closed my book and looked at her. Still in makeup, she was what passed for being pretty in California, or at least in Hollywood, for California is a very big place.

"I don't dislike you, Miss Wallace," I said.

"That's not what I asked," she said, still managing not to sound aggressive.

"You seem to resent me," she said.

"That's not completely true," I replied.

"You don't resent me?"

"You can't resent a person, Miss Wallace," I said. "You can only resent what someone does. Unless you somehow resent someone simply *being*. I don't resent you *being*, Miss Wallace. Or even being Miss Wallace.

"I'm sorry?"

"No need to be."

She paused, not quite able to work out who, if anyone, had been victorious in that exchange.

"Why haven't you spoken to me?"

"I haven't spoken to anyone," I said. "You're all very busy people, and I have nothing to do in this production."

"You act as though you want nothing to do *with* this production," she replied.

Very good, I thought.

"Now that's not strictly true," I said. "I'm very glad to have something to do with this production since the producers are paying me to be here, and paying me to live at the Biltmore. I also want the film to be a great success since I will get a percentage of the gross. So you see, Miss Wallace, I wish you no ill. None at all."

She regarded me for a moment as one might an animal one came across in the woods and didn't know whether it would flee or attack.

"You're not interested in me then?"

"No."

"I thought you might be, since I'm playing your character," she said, trying again.

"Will you sleep with me, Miss Wallace?" I asked.

She feigned indignation, but probably didn't have to try too hard.

"Certainly not!"

"Will you let me touch you?"

"No way!"

"Will you have dinner with me, Miss Wallace?" I asked again, my tone the same.

"Never!"

"Will you discuss Proust with me?" I tried.

"Why Proust?"

"It doesn't have to be Proust. Updike?"

"No."

"Well there's your answer," I said, but she looked puzzled. "Why should I be interested in *you* when you won't do any of those things with *me*?"

She stared at me for nearly a full minute, then burst out laughing. I laughed too, and it was genuine.

When the laughter subsided, she asked, "Does this mean we're friends now?"

"No."

She looked more puzzled, but now it was tinged with rising anger.

She was about to open her mouth, but the set began filling up with people for the afternoon shoot. She turned to look over the set, looked back at me briefly, then walked away.

She didn't stomp, flounce, storm, or otherwise demonstrate her anger. She simply walked away and took a seat in her chair and calmly took her script from the pouch at its side.

I admired that. I expected she'd try to speak with me again, but probably not for a month or so.

ଔ

7 August

It would be wrong to suppose that my time in Hollywood was solitary. I have a number of friends here, most of them writers out here to work on scripts. Many of them are acting as script doctors, trying to put back into stories those things that the over-paid idiots have taken out of perfectly good stories because they weren't thought to be "commercial."

We're all on the same timetable, so meals and nights were early, but the conversation was good. Script doctors can be well-paid, but they don't get screen credits, so I'm not mentioning them by name here. At least three of them were working on re-writes for *Twentieth* on a long and, according to them, shapeless script about a certain Egyptian queen. As they were all working on separate sections of it, they all professed to have no idea how it would turn out.

Someone suggested that having everyone end up dead would be a good idea.

ഇ

I knew that Norma Richards was currently working at *Metro*, but I didn't expect her to present herself outside my door at the Biltmore as she did one evening. She had just finished a day's shoot and thought she'd try to see me.

"Mr. Talmadge, I think we met a few times at parties back East. I'm Norma Richards," she said, quite modestly.

There she stood: taller than most Hollywood actresses, but very slight with only the suggestion of a figure. Wide eyes, an elegant nose and long neck, she had a beauty seldom recognized in America. Her attraction lay in her voice, the way her mouth and eyes moved, an arch of an eyebrow, in short, the ability to act for the screen.

I invited her in. She wore a summer dress and had her hair pulled back with a daisy-print headband. She had a small leather handbag and carried a pair of dark glasses.

She looked around the sitting room of my suite.

"Not very big, is it?" she said. "They should have put you up at The Ambassador, but that's Paramount for you."

She sat down in the corner of the large sofa, and I sat in a wing chair opposite.

I am in awe of few people, but she had always struck me as being wonderfully beautiful. She had a voice that was rich, aware of the meaning of the words she spoke, and well inflected, unlike so many American actresses. She also had kept her original teeth.

All the starlets when they come to Hollywood start changing themselves so that they look like every other starlet in town. They go blonde, have their noses done, their breasts enlarged and their teeth made to look like everyone else's.

I don't know what else Norma Richards might have had done, but it wasn't her teeth. They were good, but they weren't capped to that toothpaste commercial degree that made them look like a chart in a dental magazine rather than a real mouth that could kiss and speak and spit.

"What I want to know," she said, "is why Samantha Wallace is playing Marianne Phalarope and not me."

I looked at her, not yet ready to admit my total powerlessness in the situation. "Have you eaten today?" I asked her. It was only about quarter past five but if she was working, she'd be going to bed in a few hours.

"I can have something sent up," I offered. I could tell that she was uncertain about being seen with me in public. One gets sensitive to these things within about half an hour of getting to Hollywood. She was *Metro*, I was *Paramount*. It wouldn't do. Not even for a hamburger.

"I could murder a steak," she said.

I went to the telephone and called room service.

"Do you know how much I loved 'The Girl on the Train'?" she asked. "It's one of my favorite stories. Really. I'm not just trying to impress you. I read a lot of books."

She added the last line to reassure me that she wasn't just some gushing teenager.

"Kate Hepburn wouldn't have said that," I said.

"Well, in thirty years, I hope I won't have to, either," she replied. "But at my age, I bet she *did* say it."

I laughed.

"I expect you're right," I said. "But amazingly few people in this town read anything except their pay checks."

"How's the filming going?" she asked, and sounded genuinely interested.

"Well it's *something* like my story," I said.

"It's still got a train in it, then?" she said, understanding.

I laughed.

"I'm being unfair," I said. "Martin Baldwin is doing an excellent job. I expect the film will somehow succeed."

"But it's not what you wrote?"

"It's funny, but some of the changes work very well on film. They wouldn't have worked in writing, but they're visually successful."

"How do you feel about that?" she asked.

"Out of my depth."

She smiled. It was a genuine smile, with warmth, and a touch of compassion.

"Making movies is a funny business," she said. "You read something and think it would make a good picture. Then the writers try to get it to film, and find that what was brilliant in the book was either impossible to film, or just dull. That's why second-rate books make the best movies.

"Didn't you ever notice that?" she asked. "It's because their writers think so visually. First class writers aren't just visual: they talk about thoughts and motivations, fears and smells – those are things you can't film."

I thought of my other books and realized that none of them would make very good movies.

"At least you've got a good screen writer on this one," she added, helpfully. "Curtis Kavanagh is very good. He understands literary stuff, but he knows what sells tickets, too."

There was a knock on the door and a bellboy wheeled in our dinner.

We sat at the small table, which was deftly set, complete with a rose in a bud vase. A reasonable bottle of Bordeaux was produced and opened with a minimum of fuss, and two modest, but delicious steaks were uncovered along with a selection of vegetables.

Over dinner, Norma Richards reverted to Hollywood and talked about herself, the picture she was just finishing, the one she was doing next, and all the people she knew. The only questions she asked me were whether I knew the people she was talking about.

It didn't matter if I did or not, for she said what she wanted to about them anyway.

I listened to her gossip, and thoroughly enjoyed it because I spent the time imagining her as Marianne. Apart from her voice, she had bright eyes and good table manners. She ate slowly and enjoyed her food.

Over coffee, she seemed to run out of breath and names to drop, and asked if I were writing anything now. A new short story collection was at the publishers, but few people in Hollywood had any idea how long it took to publish a book.

"I'm working on a new novel, but one never knows if it will get finished," I lied.

"I hope it does."

"What else do you like reading?" I asked.

"Oh, most things," she said. "You know how boring it is making a picture. Hanging around for hours while they try to get the lighting right, or the camera not to bump into something for an important shot."

I nodded.

"Well, I like Steinbeck and Updike. I like Daphne du

Maurier," she smiled. "I'll read Agatha Christie, too. Some of the old crime stuff: Raymond Chandler."

She paused for a moment.

"Do you watch the rushes?"

"It's in my contract," I replied.

"You don't enjoy it?"

"No. I just sit there and watch twelve versions of the same three lines. If they don't actually make mistakes, I can hardly tell one from the other. At first it was interesting to see how the illusion was made. The difference between what I had watched on the set and what appeared on the screen, but the novelty wore off pretty quickly."

"I don't much like watching myself," she said. "I like doing the parts. I like seeing the stills a lot. Those are the images that last."

We'd eaten and drunk and chatted, but she never seemed relaxed. She wasn't nervous, or on edge, but I was aware that I was getting a performance, too. Was she playing Marianne, I wondered?

She might have been, but it wasn't the Marianne that I wrote any more than was Samantha Wallace's.

Once aware of this, profound disappointment filled the rest of the time Norma Richards was there. She seemed to sense that her performance had missed and subtly began to reinvent it, but without success. Still, her conversation was intelligent; her wit quick, and her presence attractive.

When she stood to go, she kissed me on both cheeks and asked, with curiosity, not malice:

"Oh, why didn't you get me to play Marianne

Phalarope? I would have loved to."

I looked at her wistfully.

"Because you're Metro and I'm Paramount."

ᏳᏰ

The following section was on pages that apparently were on the floor, while other pages in the notebook were trapped nearly vertically behind the kitchen unit. The result is that large sections of about five pages have been rendered illegible, or just rotted from the damp, or other liquids spilled over the years. Half pages exist, but they are vertical halves, and guessing the ends of lines and sentences is pointless.

ꝸꝺ

28 August

We lost nearly a day of filming today. Not that I care, apart from the fact that it lowers the profits and means I have to spend another day in this grim place. I'd rather be just about anywhere else, even Bangor. I have finally found a way of keeping from going out of my mind with boredom. I've outlined a book which has possibilities.

I managed to get all the reviews and articles out of the way, too. I don't know why my agent thinks I should continue to write those things as they have a life as long as their headlines. What do I know about other people's books anyway? Most contemporary fiction is deadly. I like William Trevor and Walker Percy, though. Percy's about as irascible as Graham Greene, though sadly, without the same depth. Percy's a one-trick pony, but it's a damn good trick.

Most distasteful was having to write about Ernest

blowing his brains out. I was besieged by reporters for comments and opinions. They didn't like my initial comment, which I thought was pretty good, but Maurice was on the phone within an hour, and I had to write a long tribute for the *Herald-Tribune* to try to repair the damage.

All I said was that to blow his brains out, Hemingway didn't need a 12-bore – a .22 would have done.

I did manage to get in the one decent first-hand anecdote that I had, which was being on a fishing trip with Ernest and John Dos Passos somewhere in the Keys. It was a ghastly day. Dos Passos and Hemingway had fallen out decades before and weren't at all glad to be in each other's company, and I was the young effete aesthete and new kid on the literary block, who knew nothing of war, nothing of big game, nothing about having a bunch of wives, and nothing about having written several dozen novels.

Anyway, we were fishing and Ernest was pulling in some prime catch – could have been anything, marlin, tuna, blue – I didn't know and didn't care. Anyway, he's got this thing half-way in when the sharks start attacking it. This sort of thing must have happened to Papa all the time (read *The Old Man and the Sea* – actually, don't bother; it's bollocks).

In a complete fury, Hem secured his rod and went below and came back with a Mannlicher-Schoenauer 6.5 and proceeded to blast at the sharks. Ended up shooting himself in the leg. The *Herald-Tribune* has the sanitized version for which they paid me quite well. That anecdote isn't in the cannon of Hemingway stories, and may just have ensured my own immortality.

I did make one outrageous prediction, though. I said that in the course of time, Hemingway's non-fiction would over-shadow his novels. His short stories were already the best of the century in American literature, but the novels were ultimately thin.

ഇ

A m*arginal note, apparently added later, read:* "Though, there is some outstanding [*underlined*] writing in *Islands in the Stream*."

ഢ

So why didn't we have the benefit of a full day's filming today? Because Mlle. Wallace was too upset. Apparently my benign presence on the set was deeply upsetting to her. I just sat there, never praising, never criticizing. She said I was like a Buddha, completely inscrutable.

I took that as a compliment. I also thought that we had come to an understanding.

Finally, after she'd spent the morning in her dressing room, Martin [*the director*] came to me and asked me to have a word with her. I responded that I had no authority whatsoever on the set, and was required by contract to be there, but not to interfere with the production.

Martin, for whom I have high regard, told me that my presence was, in fact, interfering with the production. Of course, I sensed that this might be my ticket back to civilization, and told him that, nonetheless, I was bound by the contract, and that if it were to be altered, it would need the involvement of Aram Grigoryan [*the producer*].

Unbelievably, Aram was sent for, and he asked me,

quite politely, considering the circumstances, to have a word with Mlle. Wallace.

I knocked on her dressing room door, and she invited me in – rather to my surprise.

Perhaps my opening tactic wasn't the right one.

"You know, if you don't go back on the set, neither of us gets paid."

"I don't care," was the inevitable answer.

"Well, actually, I do," I said, wandering further into her mobile dressing room and taking the comfortable chair.

"I don't know what your game is, Mr. Talmadge," she began, almost conciliatory, "but all I can tell you is that I'm scared. I'm only twenty-three, this is my first Hollywood leading part, and I actually want to do it well."

She paused for a moment, and I spoke.

"Well, this is my first Hollywood film, too," I said. "I also would like it to be a success, but did you know that I am not allowed – by contract – to interfere in any way with this production? I have been told that that extends to saying whether I am happy or not. I'm here because the pictures of me on the set make the film news. While that's good for us all, it's making you unhappy, and boring me to death."

She looked at me. I was now standing up, and, although shorter than me, I thought she might hit me.

She just stared, but I held her gaze. I was that angry, and so was she.

After a full minute, she gave a crystal laugh like I hadn't heard from her before, and extended her hand, smiling.

"Okay," she said. "We understand each other. Let's get on with it and win a few Oscars."

It was the sort of scene that in films and books lead to the two parties becoming great friends.

In truth, we barely spoke again.

☙

15 September

Well, Mlle. Wallace went back on the set and gave the director and the cast everything they could want from her performance and behavior. It still wasn't a character that I recognized, but the others were pleased. The filming continued more or less smoothly after that. I was politely ignored and left to get on with my new story.

I got on rather well with a number of the technicians on the set. They knew the score and what the arrangement was. The sound recordist and one of the senior grips used to take me drinking, and even to meet their families. Later on, I was pleased to take them all out for lunch, or go to the beach with them on the weekends we weren't filming.

George and Harry had been in Hollywood since they were teenagers. They'd had jobs at most of the studios and had seen good directors and bad, as well as bad actors and worse. While they told a few good stories, they preferred to talk about their families, baseball, fishing, going on holiday and what they'd been reading. I would match their knowledge of twentieth century fiction with any college professor's.

They had the advantage of long periods of time when they were on the set waiting for something that involved them to happen, so they read. Anything. Occasionally when writers showed up on the set, they were able to discuss – intelligently – just about anything they'd written.

So it was with me.

They liked some of my stuff and frankly said that they couldn't stand other bits. This amused me, and I was pleased to speak with them. They were well enough off, but not rich by Hollywood standards, of course, and lived in pleasant neighborhoods that no one has heard of. They had nice houses with good sized yards and small swimming pools, mortgages and wives that worked; children who had most of what they wanted, and they seemed to enjoy each other's company.

George was a second or third generation Pole, and his wife's family was Polish, too. Harry's family had been New York rag trade Jews, but they had arrived later than the ones who made it really big, but did well enough. What impressed me most was the respect and affection these two men had for each other. They'd argue about just about everything from how a scene should have been shot, about what they read, about baseball and what bait to use, yet delighted in each other's company and in the company of their families.

The wives and children, whatever their actual feelings, acted as though these other people were relatives and you couldn't do anything about it, so you got on.

It meant a lot to be included in their time together.

Over the Labor Day weekend, I joined them for a day at a small camp Harry had towards the mountains. There was a river and we fished. While not a dedicated fisherman, growing up in Maine had equipped me for just about anything that involved a fish hook, a piece of string, and fresh or salt water.

That night, we sat by a fire where we'd cooked trout and drank beer while their wives sat chatting quietly and the children argued about how much it cost to land on Pacific Avenue with two houses.

☙

27 September

The picture isn't that far behind schedule. It was a pretty easy shoot, I am told. Few location shots that required the cast, few special effects, and not too many fancy sets. Baldwin kept things moving and was very business-like in the way he directed. He was not like Hitchcock who knew exactly what he wanted before he started to shoot; Baldwin was prepared to experiment and let the leads try a few different approaches to a scene or a piece of dialogue. Occasionally, Kavanagh [*the screenwriter*] would adapt the dialogue if it were needed to fit the new approach. He did this quickly and easily, working closely with Baldwin.

I was fully prepared to be annoyed with this further shillyshallying with my story, but it was already so far from the original that it hardly mattered. Some of the new ideas they came up with were highly amusing.

There was one idea that was unfortunate. It was one of Samantha Wallace's notions and everyone was enthusiastic about it. I wasn't paying all that much attention as my book [*Alizarin Tide*] was taking shape nicely without any interruptions. In the early afternoon when they were shooting the little episode, I finally had had enough with the messing of the script.

Just when Baldwin had shouted, "Cut!" I climbed out of my high chair and shouted, at no one in particular, "Hasn't anyone here seen *Bonjour Tristesse*? Or don't you ever go to the movies?" and stomped out.

Martin Baldwin came to the Biltmore that night. It was a scene that is more comic in memory than it was at the time.

He had a bottle of decent Margaux and I immediately found a corkscrew and poured two glasses.

"I want to say," he began with disarming charm, "that I'm amazed you haven't flipped your wig before now. It can't be easy for you."

"Well, at least there weren't reporters on the set today," I said. "None of us would have come off very well."

He drank half his glass.

"As we were doing that bit, something was rattling around in my head, but I couldn't place it. Our trouble – well, *my* trouble," he continued, "is that I see too many movies. They become mixed up with scenes I'm planning, shooting, have shot. I'm sure writers have good ideas which on reflection they recognize as someone else's."

"I expect you're right," I said, not being able to think of an example.

"Anyway, thank you. You saved us some time and embarrassment. Don't worry about doing the same thing again. We should be finished shooting within two weeks. I'm sure you'll be glad to get home. Good night."

As I said, Baldwin was okay, but that didn't make me like the film any better.

☙

4 October

On a United Airlines flight from Los Angeles to Boston. Amazingly quick, these jets, but the food has already deteriorated from the DC-6 days, but I shouldn't complain, it's the fastest way home.

Filming was wrapped up on September 30. Then, there were several parties. I was compelled to throw one myself, and the good folk at the Biltmore didn't disappoint. There were speeches, reconciliations, back-slappings and enough mutual admiration to turn one into a hermit.

Not unexpectedly, the best post-picture celebration was with George and Harry. We had a barbecue at George's with the children running about and splashing everyone, and after some excellent chicken and burgers, George, Harry, several other technicians and I visited several very pleasant bars with good beer, good whisky, and good honest talk. It wasn't a binge, it was over by two a.m., but it was with friends.

The film is scheduled to open in Hollywood on March 21. It will be quite a surprise to see it, edited, with music, and as a coherent story, though I might not recognize it. I have to be there. I've already booked the Biltmore for two nights. I have no intention of staying longer than that. Fly in the day before. Watch the damn picture and fly out the next day.

It was interesting enough to see how a movie was made – if one were interested or cared. For me, it was a waste of time. Big time. Well, I drafted over a hundred pages of the new book. I think it will be a good book; not *the* book, that's still hiding in the trees ahead, but it's shaping up nicely. I decided to call it *Alizarin Sea*.[5]

I'll be glad when people stop asking me about "The Girl on the Train." It was a story. One of many. You have an idea; you see a scene, a person, you make up a bit of plot and put them all together, just as Edgar Allan Poe said. Write a few pages of dialogue that sounds convincing and you're done. A pot boiler or a work of genius – that's something that won't really be known in our lifetimes.

I found a book once that listed the best sellers for the last fifty years. There are only a handful of writers and stories that anyone has heard of today.

I'm not as conceited as people think I am. I like writing, and I'm lucky enough to have found people who will pay me to do it. It's a process that surprises me all the time, and whether what I've done is any good, I don't know. I know that stories never turn out the way I expect them to.

Sometimes the germ of the story, the character, an expression, phrase, the location – whatever it is – becomes the thing that I ultimately cut completely. I don't want to, because it's what made me start to write, but sometimes when the story's nearly done, you find it hasn't got a place in it anymore. So, you cut it. Those key sentences never again have the same power; I never feel I want to go back and write that idea again. They were a catalyst and nothing more.

I think it was Evelyn Waugh who said that he never knew how things were going to turn out. You start with a perfectly nice chap and several chapters later you find he's taken to drink. It's like that.

Still, looking over what I've written so far, poems, a poor play, several novels and a few dozen short stories, I guess what I'd like to be remembered for, if anything, is "The Girl on the Train."

☙

Here the diary ends, but the following pages are elsewhere in the notebook

❧

1 April 1962

The week from hell. There are those times when all you can do is lie in bed and wait for time to pass. The trouble is, it doesn't work. Even though you know that what's going to happen is going to be grim and grisly, you still have to get up and go through the futile motions and do the best you can.

It was with no joy that I flew to Los Angeles for the premier of *The Girl on the Train*, a film that was, allegedly, based on one of my stories. I was met at the airport by no less a personage than Aram Grigoryan, the producer of the picture. He appeared genuinely glad to see me, even though there weren't any press photographers around.

"We've got a great few days ahead, Edward," he said. Having changed my story, he obviously felt he had the same liberty to change my name.

"I'll drive you to the hotel, tell you how the premier's going to shape up," he said.

He waved to his chauffeur who collected my small suitcase and we went out to his car. It was one of those new Rolls Royces that had the twin headlamps. They spoiled the look of the cars forever.

We got in the back, which was like being in a London gentleman's club and settled in for the ride.

"Tonight, I'm having a party at my house in Beverly Hills. I'll send a car for you at seven. No need to dress up for this one. Have you got a blazer or something? That will do. You don't have to bring anything else. I know Samantha will be delighted to see you again. I tell you, I watched the whole picture again last week, and she's a sweetie. You'll love it when you see it," he said.

"By the way," he continued, "you should prepare a few comments about the film when the press asks you how you liked it after the show.

"There will be a studio lunch tomorrow at one, and then you'll have a chance to see the film in the afternoon."

"I thought I was going to see it tomorrow night," I said.

"If you don't see it before the premier, you won't be able to give your interview to the press at five," he exclaimed. "We've got the whole line up for a press conference: Samantha, Claude, Martin, you and me. Bring your tux to the studio. You won't have time to go back to the Ambassador after the press conference. We'll have sandwiches after the press conference - though the story for the press is that we're having a big dinner at one of the star's houses in Malibu."

"There is no party in Malibu?" I asked.

"Hey, there's always a party in Malibu, but we're not going to be at it."

"By the way, I'm not staying at the Ambassador. I'm

staying at the Biltmore."

"No, it's the Ambassador," Grigoryan replied and reached for his car phone.

He pushed a few numbers and then spoke.

"Carol, you booked a room for Ed Talmadge at the Ambassador, didn't you?"

He nodded.

"I thought so."

He hung up and turned to me.

"Yeah, we've booked you a room at the Ambassador."

"Maybe you have, Abraham, but I've booked one at the Biltmore and that's where I'm going to stay."

He looked at me, unsure of whether to argue about the hotel or about the fact that I'd called him by the wrong name. Like many producers, it was too much for him and he simply leaned forward, and told the driver to go to the Biltmore.

☙

I survived the party, the screening and the press conference.

Somehow.

I am glad that I had the chance to see the film before the premier as it gave me a chance to prepare my act and perfect my dialogue.

The film had a certain charm, but it wasn't anything I recognized. I saw it alone in a studio screening room, without the benefit of popcorn. To be honest, once I'd seen it, I knew I could actually enjoy watching it at the premier, as there was nothing to worry about, and nothing to do with me.

At each event, I vainly looked for George and Harry,

but they were engaged on other projects and either were working late or enjoying an early night with their families. As Aram had said, Samantha Wallace's sole aim in life appeared to be to entertain me. It was contrived that she entered Grauman's on my arm and went to the post-premier party in the car with me.

I later found out that she had broken up with her boyfriend the week before and saw that her best chance of not being seen alone was to latch on to the author. As she looked very pretty and didn't speak to me, it worked out fine.

The premier, as everyone now knows, was a triumph. The picture was going to be a smash.

There's a story about a temperamental young pianist who was recording the Beethoven fifth piano concerto with the Boston Symphony. They had to do so many takes that it over-ran the recording session by about four hours, at enormous cost. The sound men spent several days splicing endless tapes together to get a satisfactory result.

When the team met to listen to the playback, the pianist was in raptures.

"Isn't it beautiful!" he said.

"Yes," replied Erich Leinsdorf, the BSO conductor. "Don't you wish you could play that well?"

I confess to feeling like that when the thunderous applause greeted the picture credits. I was in some part responsible, but in no way was I part of what I saw. While I had moderately enjoyed the film in the afternoon, watching with an audience was wholly different. They were thrilled by what they saw; they loved Marianne

Phalarope, or Samantha Wallace – it was hard to tell which – and the poignancy of the ending left the women in tears, and even the men feeling weak.

I still like my story, but for a 0.25 percent royalty plus the generous payments already made, should I really object?

The post-premier party was in one of the older sections of Beverly Hills. It was in a house that Norma Desmond could have lived in, and had been rented by Claude Bertani. He played his part very well, and was a gracious host, paying much more attention to the guests than an American actor would have.

Today, those great houses aren't owned by actors or producers. They're owned by the studios at best, or by investment companies at worst. They have become commodities to be leased and traded and have lost their tarnished, but genuine, souls.

I stayed at the party for exactly one hour. I had two drinks – glasses of highly inferior champagne – for the studio was responsible for the catering, not Claude Bertani. Poor Claude, who doesn't drink (or seldom) wouldn't have known about the dreadful wine served in his name. The only redeeming thing was that very few of the people there would have known any different.

I managed to get a taxi back to the Biltmore.

I wasn't feeling bad, just tired. It was the end of a big adventure, and one that hadn't been altogether to my liking.

In spite of my tiredness, my mind was active, so I didn't go to bed. It was still before midnight. I finished reading the *New Yorker* and *Saturday* Review which I had started on the plane the day before, and was thinking about calling room service for a drink or an omelet when there was a knock on the door.

I opened it, and Norma Richards stood there.

"Hello, Edgar," she said. "May I come in?"

She was simply dressed in a white turtleneck jersey and a skirt. She wore sensible shoes and little make-up. No one would have picked her out as a star. She looked very appealing.

It is very pleasant to write that I spent the night with Norma Richards, but in truth, we spent the night talking, laughing, and sending down to room service for omelets, French fries, ice cream and coffee. We didn't even drink.

"I know you hate parties, so I knew you'd be here," she said. "I hate parties, too, and I thought I knew how you'd be feeling."

"After our last meeting," I began, "I never expected to speak to you again."

"This is Hollywood, Edgar. No one means what they say. Ever."

We laughed, and she asked me about the premier.

"I heard it's going to be a big hit," she said. "I hope it is."

"How can you hope it is?" I asked, in disbelief.

"Some parts you get, some you don't. I've done all right this year," she said. "You saw the picture being made. You saw all those people, all that money, all that work, all that talent. How can you not want it to succeed? Those people deserve success. They know how to make movies, and movies are entertainment for thousands – millions – of people. They're not just for those who appreciate the subtlety of language, or the nuance of a look. Those things are extras that are put in if they can be.

"Films," she continued, "have to catch the public imagination before it changes. Any number of good films have failed because they missed their moment. Fortunately, with television, they have another life; they can be seen without their immediate historical context and seen more objectively."

We continued to talk until the sun came up and then we had breakfast.

As she left, she kissed me lightly on both cheeks, and said:

"You know, Edgar, I might well be the Marianne Phalarope of your story, but I'd never have been the Marianne of the film."

☙

The entry ends there. After a few blank pages, the following note is made. It is the last entry in the notebook.

Clubs, Bills and Partisans

April 1963

The Academy Awards:

Best screenplay from another source – *The Girl on the Train*

Best original song – *The Girl on the Train*

Best director – *The Girl on the Train*

Best actress – *The Girl on the Train*

Best picture – *The Girl on the Train*

Fees and royalties to date: $1,978,237.44

The Bed

The Bed

It was his fault. She had no doubt about that, but she should have known better, she told herself.

No one called Noel should ever be trusted.

Kate could practically hear her mother saying something like that.

Oh, Noel!

Six months had passed since they broke up, and while Kate had pretty much got over the hurt, every time she thought about him, she got the same waves of hollow coldness followed by anger and self-recrimination.

She had really thought that he was the one. But, like too many others, he wasn't.

What she felt was at once deep longing and profound regret. It was the same old story. For her, for everyone. She should have seen it from the first. Men like Noel don't get married. At least not while they're still under thirty. The worst thing about it was that he had been perfectly honest.

"Do you love me?" she had shamelessly asked.

"I love you and every other pretty girl," he had answered. "I won't marry you, Katie."

He had said that days before she ever thought of it. She had taken it as a sure thing then. If he mentions marriage first, he must be serious. "Noel doth protest too much, methinks," Kate had told herself.

When she had first seen his tall, slim figure across the room at the party, she had been immediately taken with his self-assurance. The confident way he drank his tonic water; the way he spoke about doing up his flat, and colour schemes. There was nothing poofy about Noel, no question, but he was interested in things other men she had known weren't or wouldn't discuss if they were.

He was just different enough for her to be attracted more strongly than she had ever remembered being before.

And, he was smooth. His voice was like a sophisticated radio announcer's. She had told him so one afternoon after making love on the narrow bed in his undecorated bedroom in Pimlico.

"No one who is a radio announcer can be seriously considered sophisticated," he had replied.

She quoted that opinion (and others) for over a year until it became her own. Noel knew he was smooth – like Benedictine, he had once said. He had warned her about the after-effects but, again, she did not listen.

"Kate, darling. Don't try to possess me."

"Never!" she had declared, and held him more tightly.

"Don't try to change me," he had said on another occasion.

"Of course not, I love you just as you are," she had said, shortly before buying him three new jumpers and an immorally expensive pair of American designer jeans.

"I love your sense of independence," she had said, just before making him take her to the night club where everyone who was anyone had to be seen.

He had worn the jumpers and the jeans. He had gone to the night club, danced well and looked classically elegant, got his picture in *Tatler* and was picked up by a hotel heiress within hours.

Bye, bye, Kate.

He wasn't particularly wild. He was really only averagely good looking. He was moderately kind, when he wasn't preoccupied. He was generous in a way that you didn't notice. Kate had hated that at first. It was too effortless. He was smooth, though – without being oily. That was really what Noel had: charm and confidence.

"I guess he was honest, too, only I never believed him," Kate reflected.

Now, six months after their break-up, there was still one thing she wanted from him: The Bed.

It was *her* bed, even though it was at his flat. She had spotted it at the antique shop and bought it. All right, she had bought it for them, but the *them* she had bought it for was the "Kate and Noel" *them*, not the Noel and Jacqui, or Noel and Samantha, or Noel and Lynne: the *them* who had been using it since.

The Bed. Kate wasn't so far gone as to think of it as "their bed." After all, it had been someone else's bed before. Several dozen people's, in fact, if its age were anything to go by.

It was one of the most expensive things Kate had ever bought.

About two months after meeting Noel, Kate found that she had fallen into the habit of staying at his flat. Her clothes and several dozen pairs of shoes seemed to have migrated to Pimlico from Battersea. Noel's flat had a lot of room. He had two floors with space to breathe. Kate had been finding her shared flat increasingly disagreeable. Noel's flat was bright, white and clean while her own rooms were dingy, green and grubby. She would have crossed London just to use his luxury bathroom instead of her draughty damp one.

Noel let her use his tiny third bedroom as a dressing room and had provided her with a worn pine kitchen table for her mirror, makeup and array of bottles and jars. It took up a lot of room, but underneath there was room for lots of shoes.

Noel's bedroom was nearly monk-like. It was bright, but spartan. A narrow single bed without head or foot boards, a plain white melamine chest of drawers and a white bedside table with a China lamp (white, but with three thin blue lines round the base, and two blue bands on the top and bottom of the white shade) were the only furnishings. The clinical look was broken by light blue walls and carpet. Still, as a room, Kate found it wholly unappealing.

"Where do you put your things?" she had asked.

"Away," he had answered.

"What are you going to do with the room?" she had asked.

"Sleep in it."

Kate didn't believe him. But, when Noel had insisted that she put all her clothes in the tiny third bedroom before they slept together the first time, Kate did experience a twinge of doubt.

She couldn't even hang her dressing gown on the back of the door – there was no hook – and he wouldn't allow her to drop it on the floor. Still, for Noel, it had been worth it.

His narrow bed was surprisingly comfortable. It didn't sag. It didn't creak. In retrospect, this should have told her something right away, but it didn't. The bed was big enough for them, in a romantic sort of way. Kate had always dreamed of having a bed the size of a tennis court, but with Noel, it didn't seem to matter.

It was the room which bothered her. It was for the room that she had bought The Bed, not for sex or for sleeping.

At least that's what she had told Noel.

What Kate really wanted was something that was *theirs*. Something that, when they were old and remembering their first months together, they could look at and remember.

The Bed would be that thing.

Like all special beds, it wasn't extraordinary.

They were walking home from a party in Chelsea when Kate spotted it in a window. It wasn't The Bed which attracted her attention, but a statue of a moor holding a torch in the Venetian fashion, it was in excellent condition except that someone, owner or vandal, had painted the whole thing bright red.

The Bed stood, dismantled, behind the figure, and it was its broken carving that Kate first noticed. The headboard had carved medallions on it; garlands and wreaths, boldly cut, but fine and tasteful. She pointed it out to Noel.

"I've got a bed, but it has possibilities," Noel said.

Kate, undeterred, said nothing, but after work the next day went to the shop to have a closer look. It was covered with a heavy dark varnish which was cracked with age. Some of the carving was damaged, but not as badly as she had thought. The man in the shop even had some of the broken bits.

Kate considered it as she saw its pieces brought from the window for her inspection. She didn't think Noel would ever have it in the house in its present state. She would have to have it delivered to her own flat.

"We don't deliver," said the man. "This ain't Harrods."

Kate pleaded, but the man wasn't going to break the habit of a lifetime for her. She went to a call box and rang Noel.

"You really want that bed, don't you?" he asked.

"Noel, it's perfect! I mean, it needs a lot of work, but it will be splendid!"

The silence at the end of the phone had frightened her.

"Put a deposit on it. I'll meet you at the shop at four-thirty."

"Wonderful, darling!" she cried into the phone, but he had hung up.

At four-thirty, Noel had rolled up with car and The Bed and all its bits were moved out of the shop and strapped to the roof-rack. Inside, Kate was writing the cheque.

"Wait, Kate," Noel said. "Let's split it."

Kate thought that this was the first really romantic thing that Noel had done. However, by now, she had learned not to say anything about it. He would only spoil it by saying something like, "Well, you're only going to sleep in half of it."

It was unusable in its current state, so it was moved to a back room where it could be worked on.

To Kate's surprise, Noel began to work on it with alacrity. She never would have guessed from the plainness of his furnishings that he could refinish furniture as easily as he could. He also cut a large number of slats.

Within a matter of weeks, The Bed was repaired, stripped, oiled and polished. Every detail of the simple carvings glowed. For herself, Kate had been to the shops and bought a spring and mattress, sheets and pillow cases, and a double duvet and cover.

When they moved the small single bed from his room, Kate had wanted to throw it away or sell it, but Noel insisted on putting it in the spare room.

"Friends expect beds these days," he said. "They seem to have outgrown sleeping on the floor after parties."

The Bed had served them well, Kate reflected. It had been their first purchase. As it happened, it was their only purchase. The Bed, had already outlasted several generations, so it was hardly surprising that it outlasted them, though Kate had not expected to break up with Noel eight months after The Bed was installed.

The Bed, or bed generally, had nothing to do with their parting. Noel had simply said that she was crowding him, and he didn't wish to be crowded. The heiress was incidental.

Kate couldn't cope with the feeling that everything she said was being judged and, although they continued to share The Bed, they saw less and less of each other, until Kate decided that she might as well go back to Battersea.

She made the decision calmly enough. It wasn't until the bottom fell out of the cardboard box containing all her shoes, depositing them in the gutter, that she could no longer preserve the façade of detachment and inevitability.

For all of its pain, it had been a very clean break. Kate went through her usual progression from feeling cheap and used to simple desolation, then to affected hate, anger, indifference and irritation. It was while in the irritated stage, six months later that she began to think about The Bed again in objective terms.

"I want it back!" was the objective way she phrased it to herself.

She had not seen or spoken to Noel – *Noel!* – since she had collected her things. It took a great deal of courage (some of it Dutch) for her to dial his number.

"Noel? This is Kate."

Please don't let him say, "Kate who?"

"Hello, Kate."

"Noel, I want The Bed back."

There was silence.

"Noel?"

"Yes?"

"I want The Bed back."

"I heard you."

"You didn't say anything."

"You didn't ask anything."

Kate resisted the urge to slam the phone down.

"Well?"

"Well, what?"

"Can I have it back?" she asked, trying to sound business-like and not niggled.

"Which half do you want?"

"What?"

"Half of it is mine."

"Right. I'll buy you out. Half of six hundred pounds is a three hundred – "

"It's worth more now, refinished. I could get over a thousand for it, easily."

"I'm surprised you haven't."

"I still need a bed."

"I'll give you four hundred."

It was a reckless offer, and one she could ill afford, but Noel was right: it would fetch far more now in the right place.

"Wait, a minute – " she interrupted herself. "I bought the spring and mattress myself not to mention the duvet and sheets."

"I refinished it. You wouldn't want it now if it hadn't been refinished. Would you?"

She didn't answer. Damn!

"Five-fifty. No more."

"Done," he said, without emotion.

"Can you drive it round?" she asked.

"No."

"You lazy sod! I'm paying you – "

"You want it, you collect it. This ain't Harrods," he said, flatly.

It had been their joke about The Bed, and hearing it like that hurt.

"I'll need to borrow your car," she said. "Mine's not big enough and you have the roof-rack."

She knew better than to ask. Simply informing him was the best policy.

"I'll collect it around three on Thursday."

"Suit yourself," was all he said.

"Bastard!" she exclaimed, but not before she hung up.

She took the underground, which she hated. She hated the idea of seeing Noel, but it couldn't be helped if she wanted The Bed. She had avoided going to Pimlico at all since breaking up, even though it meant driving miles out of her way. She even missed the exhibition of her favourite painter.

Noel's flat was a ten minute walk from the station.

When she arrived at the flat, Noel answered with a curt, cold, "Hello, here are the car keys," then turned back up the stairs. He wouldn't fetch the car with her, and it was with difficulty that she manoeuvred it out of the narrow garage and turned from the alley.

She pulled up in front of the door, parking half on the pavement half on the double yellow lines and went in to collect her bed. Noel's interest in the transaction had only extended to leaving the door on the latch for her.

The Bed was just barely made, and it was with considerable distaste that she stripped it of its Shalimar-smelling sheets and packed them into a black bin-liner she had brought for the purpose.

"Can you help with the mattress?" she asked.

He helped her downstairs with all the pieces, slats and frame, and secured it to the rack.

"You could at least be nice to me," Kate said.

"Your phone call wasn't exactly friendly."

"No. I suppose it wasn't. I had got myself worked up about The Bed. I didn't expect it to smell of perfume, though."

"No, you wouldn't have."

"Shalimar, for God's sake. I am disappointed, Noel."

"Kate," he said, in voice dying of boredom, "just take the bed and don't criticise my girlfriend."

Kate reached for her cheque-book and felt her hand tremble. She hadn't reckoned on a new woman. She was even more shocked by what he said next.

"I hope you and your new man make good use of it."

Unable to utter a sound, Kate handed over the cheque and got into the car. It took several attempts to get it started. She glanced up at the house, but Noel had shut the door, too indifferent to gloat over her mortification.

It was the rush hour. Traffic stood motionless in long queues and Kate's fury grew. Why couldn't he see that it wasn't just The Bed that I wanted? It was only special because of us. It's just a bed that I haven't the money to pay for or the room to put it in. It was our bed, it reeks of Shalimar now and who knows what he's been up to in it and with whom.

The sod! How could he so calmly help me out of the door with it?

A taxi honked at Kate. She popped the clutch and stalled. The taxi honked again.

"It's just a bloody bed," she shouted in response to the taxi. "Oh, the hell with it."

At the next intersection, she turned and headed back to Noel's. She parked half on the pavement and stomped up to the door and held her finger on the bell.

Noel appeared very quickly.

Before he could speak, Kate walked past him and went up the stairs. Noel followed. She faced him in the sitting room.

"You can have the bed. I've decided that I don't particularly want to be reminded of you every night. You obviously have more use for it than I do with your little Miss Shalimar-Sheets, which, by the way, the whole car smells of now – anyway, you can have the damn thing and give me my cheque back."

Noel said nothing, but took the cheque from his desk drawer and gave it to her. Kate tore it up and dropped the pieces in the fireplace.

"You never did know what you wanted," Noel said.

"Well, I do now," Kate answered, and headed down the stairs.

"Hey! Aren't you going to help bring the bed up?"

"This ain't Harrods."

She slammed the door in answer. Outside, some men were preparing to work down a manhole.

"Is this your car, lady?" one of them asked.

"No."

"Does the owner live there?" the man asked. "If he moved it in the next two minutes, we wouldn't have to have it towed."

"No idea. I've never seen it before in my life."

The Valentine Hop
A Westbury Tale

The Valentine Hop
A Westbury Tale

January & February 1967

Nick was waiting in front of Dexter's in late January. It was dark, cold, and the slush had soaked through his shoes. Snow that afternoon had slowed Westbury to a crawl. While the main streets had been sanded and plowed, streets beyond the city center were becoming treacherous. As a result, the buses were running way behind schedule.

"Where's everyone else?" Stu Gardner asked, coming up and stamping his feet. "Did you get sent home early, too?"

"Yeah. The Academy closed right after lunch, but buses were having trouble on the hill so I walked down," Nick said. "I think I've got frostbite. Where's Buzz?"

"He went home at lunchtime. He didn't want to risk his knee," Stu said.

They stood there watching their breaths blow into the snow that was gusting under the department store's marquee.

"Want to get a coffee or hot chocolate?" Stu asked.

Stu never suggested such things, so Nick knew something must be on his mind. The two had known each other since grade school, then junior high. In their sophomore years, Stu had gone to St. Benedict's and Nick had gone to Westbury Academy.

"Shall we go to Ernie's Kitchen?" Stu suggested.

Ernie's was open six to six; you could get the full menu all day at the same prices – until they ran out of something. It was a place popular with business men, workers from the retail stores and machine shops, and there were always some police and firemen in there, too.

The place had been "Ernie's" father's. He was the real "Ernie," who had opened it in 1932. The current owner was his son, Benny, but with his father gone, everyone called him "Ernie."

"There are worse things to be called," Benny/Ernie would say. "I'm proud of my dad."

His dad was proud of him, too. Benny had won a Silver Star in WWII and only started cutting sandwiches and making soup when he couldn't find work at the end of the war.

Ernie's Kitchen wasn't fancy, but it was spotless and there were no short-cuts.

Stu and Nick went in and found a table by the steamy plate glass window that looked out onto the sloppy street. Within a minute a waitress came by and took our orders for coffee and Boston cream pies. It was a luxury.

"Everything okay?"

Stu moved his head around indicating yes and no.

"Basically okay, but complications on the horizon," he said.

The food arrived. Whatever was on Stu's mind could wait until he'd had a piece of his pie.

"I was out shopping yesterday at the mall with Buzz and a few others from school. We'd talked about going to a movie but, well, didn't. While arguing about which film to see, a bunch of girls came out of the earlier showing. Laura was with them, so that meant that she and Buzz only talked to each other.

"We were talking to the other girls, when Elisabeth Western came up to me. This was a bit strange, because I don't really know her. We talked about the movie, which she said wasn't worth seeing, and then she asked me to the Valentine Hop at Pinehill."

"That was fast work!" Nick exclaimed. "You weren't going with anyone else, were you?"

"No," he said, putting his fork down.

"Waiting for someone to ask you?" Nick persisted.

"No. I was expecting to give this one a miss. It seems way too serious – and too sappy."

"I know what you mean," Nick agreed. "Still, girls ask boys who are just friends to it. Patricia and I are more friends than anything. And Buzz and Laura? Is that really serious? They certainly have fun together, but is it romantic?"

"Yeah. You're right," he said. "It was just such a surprise. I mean, why me?"

"So, did you say yes?"

"She said she knew she'd ambushed me and gave me until tomorrow to let her know," Stu said. "She's going to be at Susan's and I'm supposed to call her there."

"Why there?" Nick asked.

Stu sighed.

"It's her mother. She's very protective and doesn't want her getting calls from boys."

"What do you want me to say?" Nick asked.

"She's a bit odd, isn't she?" he asked, at length.

"Her mother?"

"No! Elisabeth."

"Quiet. Maybe shy, but not while playing field hockey. She's reckoned to be deadly."

"Yeah. Releasing her pent-up murderous frustrations."

"Look, Stu. Bottom line: do you like her enough to endure an evening with her? The music will be loud enough so you won't have to listen to her much."

He finally smiled.

"You're right. It could be fun," he admitted.

"You'll have enough friends around you to stop her if she suddenly pulls out a chainsaw."

ஐ

Nick told Patricia Stu's story when he telephoned her that evening. He also asked how well she knew Elisabeth.

"She's a bit of a dark horse, I think," Patricia said. "I'm surprised she invited Stu."

"Why? What's wrong with Stu?"

"Nothing," she said, defensively.

"Is she doing this to play some trick on him? I don't want to see him messed about."

"No. Nothing like that. Elisabeth is, shall we say, *sensitive*. She takes things very personally – good things and bad," she continued. "I think she chose him because she likes him and thinks he's funny, but also because she believes that beneath the clowning, there's someone sensitive and kind."

Nick said nothing.

"I know," Patricia said. "It sounds feeble, but I think it's probably true."

"I don't know about Stu being sensitive, but he's basically kind. He's a decent guy. He's been a good friend."

"Exactly," Patricia said. "Elisabeth hasn't gone out much. I hate saying things like this, but she's a bit socially awkward. I mean, she doesn't eat peas with her knife, but she's not used to being around boys."

Nick considered this.

"She told Stu to call her tomorrow evening at Susan's," he said. "Don't you think that's odd – not to give him her telephone number?"

Patricia didn't reply immediately.

"I think her mother is pretty old-fashioned and strict," she said. "I don't know that much – I'm not sure anyone does, maybe Susan – but she and her mother are on their own, and where they live is pretty remote."

"You're making it sound creepy."

"Look, Nick," Patricia said, in her school council chairman's voice, "you're obviously gathering intelligence for Stu. So, I'll tell you this: if he goes to the dance with her, he'll have a great time; she cleans up well, and she's not stupid. No one will tease Stu or her about it because they know she'll cream them in the next sporting event."

"What – ?"

"No, that's all you'll get from me. Call Stu and tell him it could be a really great move for both of them. I'm going to do my math homework."

"But Patri – "

"Girls don't like talking to their boyfriends about other girls," she cut him off, but it sounded more like a joke than a serious admonition. "Call me tomorrow when Stu's got himself sorted out."

ꟹ

Nick called Stu, who had already come to the conclusion that, as long as he wasn't being set up, he had little to lose.

"I'll call Susan tomorrow," he said.

"Is she going with anyone?"

"I don't know for sure. Bill Patterson, maybe."

"And Buzz? Did Laura ask him?"

"Oh, yes," Stu laughed. "They're the hot new comedy team."

"Let me know how you get on."

☙

It wasn't until the end of the week that Nick saw Stu again, under Dexter's marquee. By then, Susan had told Patricia, and she had told him; Claire had told Tom, and Amy had told John.

Buzz and Stu stumbled off the bus from school. Buzz was trying to move carefully from bus steps to the icy sidewalk while Stu was trying to push forwards to see Nick. Their book bags tangled and while Buzz was able to descend successfully, Stu slipped on the ice and for a moment looked like a silent movie character trying to retain his balance, which he eventually did. Four of his awaiting friends applauded.

He ignored them and walked up to Nick.

"Coffee?"

"Sure."

They took the same seats at Ernie's Kitchen and ordered the same things as before. Stu hadn't said anything since leaving the front of Dexter's. Again, Stu waited until they'd been served before speaking.

"Well, it's done."

"So I've heard," Nick said.

Stu laughed.

"I suppose that's inevitable," he said.

"She was happy you agreed?"

"You could say that."

He drank some coffee and continued to warm his hands on the mug.

"I called Susan who passed the phone to Elisabeth as soon as she said hi. I had rehearsed one stupid phrase for nearly twenty-four hours, but still managed to blow it."

"What did you say?"

"I had planned to say, 'I'd be happy to go to the dance with you.' Not hard, is it? Well, I started by saying, 'Thank you for asking me,' which she took as the preamble to a rejection, so I had to fix that in a hurry and said, 'It would be great to go with you.'"

"Not super-cool, but it does the job," Nick said.

Elisabeth said nothing, and I'd recovered enough to say, 'Thank you for inviting me,' but she'd given the phone back to Susan. She just said, 'It's me again.'

"I asked where Elisabeth had gone, and was anything wrong? Had she changed her mind?"

Nick gave a quizzical look.

"Yeah. A bit odd," Stu agreed. "Susan's voice dropped to a near whisper and said, 'I can't say more now, but you've made a young lady very happy.'"

Nick could see how much this had affected Stu, as he hadn't touched his pie.

That evening, Nick called Patricia. He expected her to be out, about to go out, or otherwise engaged, but she was there and willing to talk.

He told her what Stu had said, and asked what he was supposed to read into that reaction.

"You boys think everything is easy for us," she said, almost with weariness. "I'll tell you what I know, but you must promise not to tell Stu. He may find out anyway, but Susan said she'd only told me.

"So, will you promise?"

The tone of her voice told him that this was serious.

"I can't promise if it's something that will hurt Stu. Guy's have loyalty, too," he said.

Patricia laughed easily, which Nick had not been expecting.

"No," Patricia said, still laughing. "Stu is in no danger."

Nick remembered his crack about a chainsaw.

"Okay, I trust you," she said, finally. "You've kept my big secret so far, so I'll trust you with this.

"This is Elisabeth's first date."

Nick was incredulous.

"Really? She's a senior! Why? What's wrong with her? Does she smell? Doesn't she like guys?" he blurted.

"Nothing's wrong with her. She's just been pretty sheltered, just her and her mother out in the sticks," Patricia began. "Unless you're in town, it's not all that easy to meet boys if you're at a girls' school. She doesn't even get to see them on the bus, like we do.

"Her mother always drove her until last spring and she drives now, but goes right home," she continued. "So, not only can she not telephone boys, she can't drive them, either."

Neither of those rules was unusual, which is what made waiting under Dexter's marquee something of a social clearing house. The only other opportunities to mix at Westbury's single-sex schools was doing drama, or singing. Elisabeth's field hockey didn't attract a significant following – usually, only the boyfriends of the girls playing would watch the matches.

"The truth is," Patricia continued, in an even lower voice, "that when Stu said he'd go with her, she burst into tears and gave the phone back to Susan."

This was so far from the way Nick and his friends thought girls behaved as to render him speechless.

"She's not going to go all *Star Trek* on him, is she?"

"What?"

"Klingon. We've all seen girls like that drive guys away because they stick to them like flypaper," he said.

"Who did that?" Patricia asked, sounding amused. "I never knew anyone like that."

"That Rubenesque piece of work from Big Hair, New Jersey. Drove Steve Crespi nuts."

"Oh! Vivica. I'd forgotten her!" she laughed. "Yes, she was – er – *different*."

Nick was laughing now. When they recovered, Patricia spoke reassuringly.

"Stu has nothing to worry about. Susan and I are going to have everything under control, and you can help," she said. "We thought it would be a good idea to have a group date before the dance. Let them get to know each other. Next Saturday would be good. The eleventh. Maybe at Sillitoe's. Susan can't make it, but we could get Laura and Buzz and you and me."

"Sure. Buzz and Stu will keep Elisabeth entertained, that's for sure."

"Okay. Can you check with Stu and Buzz and I'll talk to Elisabeth and Laura," she said. "Stu doesn't have to ask Elisabeth. We'll put it to them as I just suggested it: a good idea for a simple group date."

ↂ

All the parties knew that there is no such thing as a "simple group date," but somehow, the pieces are assembled and quite a few of them do happen successfully. Sillitoe's was about as unthreatening a place as could be found in Westbury. It had only been open a year or two and was in a rehabbed machine shop with sandblasted walls and ceiling, bits of old equipment and a limited menu. During the day it operated as a coffee and sandwich shop, but in the evenings, there was a limited hot menu, and sometimes music or poetry readings.

On the fourth, it was quiet. Some Christmas music still played intermittently, but the tape would run out and no one would turn it over, sometimes for more than an hour.

Nick and Patricia were the first ones there and were reading the menu over glasses of soft drinks when Laura arrived.

"She's not going to come," Nick said.

"It's just as likely that Buzz and Stu will be the ones not to show up," Laura said, with impatience. "Clowns."

"I don't care if they come or not," Nick said. "I'm hungry."

Buzz and Stu were late, which was to be expected, but there was no sign of Elisabeth, either.

"Susan said she was pretty nervous about this," Laura said. "She doesn't like misleading her mother."

"Why couldn't she just tell her?"

Laura and Patricia looked at each other.

"You haven't met Mrs. Western," Patricia said, quietly.

"Well, where does she think Elisabeth's going to be next Saturday night, dressed to go to a dance?"

"That's why she dared to ask Stu to the Valentine Hop – she won't have to be all that dressed up," Laura said.

"It's not going to be good for Stu when Mrs. Western finds out," Nick said.

They were distracted from their conversation by a commotion at the door and a good deal of laughter.

Stu, Buzz and Elisabeth pushed through the door like the Marx Brothers or The Three Stooges, each trying to get in first. Elisabeth made it in first, then they argued until after they sat down about whether the boys had let her in or if she had outmaneuvered them.

Patricia, Laura and Nick couldn't help but laugh as the argument continued. When it did, Buzz explained:

"We met in the car park," Buzz said. "We've been talking out there for about ten minutes."

Elisabeth looked bemused, but hadn't said anything since they sat down. Nick watched them as the conversation continued, with Patricia and Laura joining in. Although Elisabeth looked animated, she said nothing.

A waitress came to take their orders. They all ordered lasagna. Buzz and Stu ordered French fries with theirs.

As prearranged, Buzz turned his attention to Laura, which wasn't difficult for him to do, while Patricia and Nick chatted with them, or by themselves. This was contrived to make Stu and Elisabeth talk to each other, though Laura and Buzz, who were next to them, did their best to listen.

Nick and Patricia exchanged looks at different times as Stu and Elisabeth seemed to be getting on well. Elisabeth never said much, but smiled a lot and made encouraging comments. Buzz and Laura seemed to have given up listening and were engage in their own lively, and sometimes boisterous flirtation.

By the end of the evening, what was noticeable was that Stu had his open hand on the table and Elisabeth was resting hers on top of it, occasionally brushing it in different directions as they talked quietly.

At one point, over dessert, Stu suddenly reacted to something loudly.

"*What?!*"

The others stopped talking and looked towards Elisabeth and Stu in time to see her jerk her hand away and her eyes fill with tears.

"Hey! What's the matter?" Laura demanded, looking at Buzz and then at Elisabeth.

It was instantly clear that Stu's reaction had been one of surprise, not anger.

"Elisabeth just told me she hadn't told her mother she was going to the dance," he said, sounding bewildered. "She said I'd have to go meet her mother first. I mean, the dance is a week tonight."

"We all know that Stu's a bit of a goof, but he's harmless enough," Buzz said. "Maybe someone else could go in his place."

It didn't seem to help.

Tears were now trickling down Elisabeth's face, and she made no attempt to control them or wipe them away. She sat there, an almost neutral expression on her face.

"I'm sorry guys, Elisabeth," Stu said. "I didn't mean to stop the party. I was surprised."

"When would your mother like to meet Stu?" Laura asked calmly.

Elisabeth finally reached into her bag and drew out a handkerchief.

"She's back at six on Tuesdays and Thursdays," she said, almost in a whisper. "It doesn't matter. Stu won't want to go with me now."

Before anyone realized it, she was standing up and putting on her coat. She turned to Stu, then to the others.

"Thank you for trying," she said, and put ten dollars on the table. Then, turning to Stu, the tears returning, "I'm sorry I spoiled your evening."

She was at the door before Stu was on his feet, nearly knocking the chair over, and he followed her out.

The four looked at each other.

"What happened?" Patricia asked Laura and Buzz.

Laura shook her head.

"It seemed to be going so well, then all of a sudden, he reacts and she bursts into tears," she said. "It was pretty insensitive of Stu, but I guess I should have expected something like that."

"Hey, wait a minute! Have you told your parents you invited me to the dance?" Buzz demanded.

"Of course, I have," Laura snapped.

"Have you told yours you're going with Nick?" he asked Patricia.

"They'd be surprised if I wasn't going with him," she said.

"Your parents know?" Buzz asked Nick.

"Well, yeah."

"And so do mine – they question my taste, but they always have," he added, just to show Laura he wasn't too pissed off. It didn't provoke a laugh, but she didn't throw anything.

"So, how do you think Stu felt?" he asked, with the flourish of a television lawyer. "Are you really surprised he reacted? *'What?!'* is pretty mild when you consider the alternatives."

The waitress came to ensure that no one else left before she brought the bill. Buzz ordered more coffee and the others ordered coffee, too, or hot chocolate, and waited for Stu to come back.

It was nearly another ten minutes before Stu returned – alone – and looking very confused.

Buzz, for once, didn't have a sarcastic remark.

"You okay?" he asked, with genuine concern.

He nodded.

"What just happened?" Nick asked.

Stu shook his head slowly.

"I wish I knew."

He waved to the waitress and asked for another coffee.

"When I followed her out to her car, I thought she was going to spend the next two days shouting at me, but she apologized, and the tears started again.

"Man! I can take a lot, but not tears. Anything but tears," he said, and put his head in his hands.

"What did she say?"

He didn't look up until his coffee came.

"Hardly anything," he said. "I said I was sorry if I upset her, and she said it was her fault. She said she was new at this, and to please be patient with her.

"I'd never heard that one before," he said, with incredulity.

"You're not alone in that," Buzz said.

"Then, she said that not only had she not told her mother about the dance, but that her mother thought Elisabeth was at Laura's this evening!"

"That's my fault," Laura confessed.

"What's the matter with her mother?" Buzz asked.

"Anyway," Stu continued, "I asked what was wrong with me that she was afraid to tell her mother."

His head hung.

"What did she say?" Laura asked.

Stu looked up.

"She started crying again," he said. "It's not really crying. She doesn't sob, she just – *weeps*. Buckets."

He sat back in his chair, looking like he'd just completed fifteen rounds with someone out of his league.

No one said anything until Laura spoke.

"So, is the dance off?"

Stu sat up looking shocked.

"Hell, I hope not! I think she's terrific."

༄

What followed would have been a good plot for a teen movie.

Laura, Susan and Patricia surrounded Elisabeth at lunch the following Monday.

"Do you want to go to this dance?" Laura asked, in her no-nonsense way.

Taken off guard, she dropped her fork, looking like a deer in the headlights. ("Better that than road-kill," Nick said to Patricia when she related the scene.)

Gathering her wits, Elisabeth nodded and mouthed, "Yes. Very much."

"That's good. After Saturday, Stu wasn't sure."

"Why would he still want to?" Elisabeth asked.

"God knows," Laura retorted. Elisabeth looked down. "But he does. Very much. He likes you."

Elisabeth looked at the three girls. The dam was still holding, but its condition looked dubious.

"Elisabeth, what has to happen for this to work out the way you want it to?" Patricia asked. "Susan is not going to cover for you again."

"Stu has to be able to come around to see you once in a while, at least to pick you up," Susan added.

Water was about to spill over, but Elisabeth just shook her head slowly.

༄

Nick telephoned Patricia Tuesday evening. He had seen Stu on the way home from school on Monday and Tuesday. To say he was confused was an understatement. He had not heard from Elisabeth since Saturday night.

Nick told Patricia this, and she and her friends had come up with a plan.

"Call Stu and tell him that Laura, Susan and I will pick him up at St. Benedict's tomorrow," she began. "We'll go to Elisabeth's house – all of us – and talk to Elisabeth's mother.

"Elisabeth has some sports' meeting after school, so we can get there first."

"I'm sure Stu will appreciate your support, but what is this supposed to achieve?" Nick asked.

"We're going to end the charade and introduce her to Stu and tell her that while he can come across as goofy, he's actually a decent guy who we have all known for ages to no ill effect," she said.

"Stu will tell her that he can either pick up Elisabeth, or meet her at Pinehill," Patricia continued. "We'll brief him fully on the way. All you have to do is be sure he waits for us at school. We'll pick him up."

Nick considered this.

"This is daft," he said, then paused again.

"Nick?" Patricia asked after more than a minute.

"What do *you* think of Elisabeth?" he asked. "I'll tell you what *I* think: I don't know her. I think she's attractive, but I also think she's a fruitcake."

Now, Patricia went quiet.

"And don't give me that line about talking to boys about other girls again," Nick prompted.

"You'd think that someone so aggressive on the field would be confident in the classroom and socially," Patricia eventually said.

"That doesn't answer my question."

"Before this, we only spoke occasionally. She's nice enough, but even if she sits with us in the cafeteria, she says nothing."

"What are her grades like? Where does she want to go to college?" Nick asked.

"She hasn't said," Patricia said. Then, after a pause, she added, "Look, there's no law that people have to tell you everything. She's entitled to her privacy."

After another long pause, Patricia asked, "I'm going to ask you the same question. What are your impressions after Saturday. Do you still think she's a fruitcake?"

"What the hell?" Nick began. "Okay. I think she's attractive without being pretty. She's really tall. I hadn't taken that in before. Must be at least five-nine. She didn't seem to have much conversation with the rest of us, but she and Stu seemed to do all right, though there were a lot of long pauses. Then that bizarre hand business. I thought she was about to go into a Vulcan death grip.

"I had the chance to look at her at Sillitoe's and don't take this the wrong way – she's got lovely eyes, when they're not full of water, but they are impossible to read."

Patricia's mood had lightened, and she was giggling now.

"I know exactly what you're saying," Patricia agreed. "Forget about eyes being windows to the soul, hers *are* beautiful, but opaque. I can never tell what she's really thinking."

"Maybe that's part of her attraction," Nick mused. "It's like looking at a living portrait."

Patricia gave a little gasp.

"That's so weird!" she exclaimed. "I thought that the other night, too! I decided that she had a face like a Renaissance portrait: well-proportioned with high cheek-bones, a strong nose, naturally colored skin, and her hair falls in a way that enhances the shape of her face."

"Wow! You are waxing poetic," Nick laughed.

"Okay, Nick," she said, coming back to normal. "Just call Stu."

ઌ

It wasn't difficult to persuade Stu to fall in with the plan. He complained of it being embarrassing, clumsy, and he worried that it would be talked about at both schools for months to come.

"Well, I'm leaving in June, so, screw it," he said.

He also agreed, without protest, to storm the citadel, beard the wicked witch in her lair and free the princess.

Nick was standing under Dexter's marquee late Wednesday afternoon when Buzz and Stu got off their bus. Without a word, Stu pointed to the side street, indicating that another trip to Ernie's Kitchen was in order.

This time, Buzz went with them.

"How's the leg, Buzz?"

"This damp cold still makes it ache, but the movement is fine and I've got most of the strength back," he said. "It's funny, you get the cast off and you think everything's back to normal. It takes *months*!"

"Buzz knows the whole humiliating story," Stu said. "I didn't want to talk about yesterday's escapade all day, so he doesn't know that bit yet."

"You appeared to survive," Nick said.

Stu smiled.

"It was fine in the end," he said. "I never expected to have three girls argue my cause, but they were all great."

They found places at the café and, as usual, Stu waited until we had been served before he continued.

"Susan, Laura and Patricia did all the talking," he resumed. "They'd rehearsed things well and handed off to each other very convincingly.

"First, they talked about Elisabeth's rising popularity at the school, from her sports, then from her academic work, then for her quiet kindness. Mrs. Western was pleased to hear all this, but started to wonder why I was there.

"Next, they talked about the dances and the importance of having a good final few months of school. 'Making good memories,' is what Susan called it.

"Finally, they mentioned the dance and how I wanted to go with her – they played down the bit where *she* asked *me*."

"What an operator!" Buzz said, while Stu attacked his pie.

"The next bit was hard," Stu continued. "Mrs. Western began talking about all the people in her life that she had lost: her older brother, her husband, and another good friend – all within a few years. She said she was trying to protect Elisabeth from unnecessary pain until she left school.

"'But do you think she's a happy girl?' Patricia asked. That was pretty ballsy," Stu said, "but, you know, Mrs. Western admitted that she might not be."

He stopped as Nick and Buzz were leaning forward in anticipation of the outcome. Stu was considering something, then ate some more pie.

"It was Laura who put the screws in," he said, when he'd swallowed. "She said, 'Doesn't Elisabeth deserve to have the things you had before they were lost?'"

He shook his head in admiration.

"That was deep," Buzz said, without irony.

"What did Mrs. Western say?"

Stu sat back.

"That's when the whole scene changed. Elisabeth drove up and walked in. She started to smile at the girls, saw me, burst into tears and ran upstairs."

"Great timing," Buzz said.

"What did you do?" Nick asked.

"Well, ordinarily, I would have followed her, but that wasn't going to work. We all looked at each other, then Patricia asked if she should go up. Mrs. Western shook her head and went up herself.

"I have to say, I thought we might as well pack up and go home," Stu said. "But, in a few minutes, Mrs. Western came back down with Elisabeth.

"They sat together on the sofa. I was looking at Elisabeth, but she hardly dared to look at me. She was mortified, red with embarrassment and clearly terrified about what would happen next.

"That's when I deviated from the script," Stu said. "Laura looked like she was going to kill me, but I asked Mrs. Western if I could speak to Elisabeth on the porch."

"That was a gamble," Buzz said. "You appear to have survived."

"Mrs. Western surprised all of us and said, 'That's up to Elisabeth.'

"We went onto the porch and sat in two chairs away from the living room windows. I asked her if she still wanted to go to the dance with me. Before she could answer, I said that I still very much wanted to go with her."

"Well played!" Nick said. "I couldn't have done that."

Stu gave one of his cheeky smiles.

"Sometimes I surprise myself."

When Buzz and Nick finished deriding him, Buzz asked what Elisabeth had said.

"Absolutely nothing. She just turned on the waterworks, again."

"That could get old," Buzz said.

"Yes," Stu agreed. "One day, but not yet.

"I was trying not to be mean, but I wanted more," he said. "So I asked, 'Is that a yes?' When she didn't answer, I stood up. With a second she was standing close to me – very close – touching my sweater on my arms, and gently tugging the wool. She looked at me with those impenetrable eyes and gave the slightest of nods.

"As I turned to go back in, she briefly touched my hand, and I knew everything would be all right."

"Depends on your definition of all right," Buzz said.

Stu shot him an impatient look, but said nothing.

"Mrs. Western agreed, but said that either Elisabeth would drive herself, or she would take her," he said. "I can live with that. Their place is a pig to find."

ᢀ

The Pinehill Valentine Hop was supposed to be informal. Although it took place in the same hall as the Holly Ball, there were few decorations, basic food, and it was a sock hop.

The sock hop was a hangover from the fifties, but it was still popular at Pinehill, so it continued. The idea of a sock hop was that shoes weren't worn to protect the floors of school gymnasiums where they were usually held. There would be a small live band, and being a Valentine's dance, there would be more slow songs than fast ones.

It was the last chance for Pinehill girls to invite boys to a school dance and all of them hoped to convert that investment into an invitation to a prom at the Academy or St. Benedict's.

Consequently, few observed the relaxed dress requirements: basically, anything except jeans and T-shirts was acceptable. The reality was, the girls dressed well, and gave their dates a preview of what their makeup at a prom would look like, while the boys might wear chinos, but most would wear a jacket albeit without a tie. They also knew the value of securing a prom date.

When Patricia and Nick approached the entrance to the hall, they found Stu waiting in the cold.

"You should wait inside," Patricia said. "Elisabeth isn't going to want to dance with a popsicle."

"Buzz and Laura here yet?" Nick asked.

"No."

"I bet Elisabeth went to Laura's first," Patricia said. "They'll all arrive together."

Nick took Patricia's arm and led her inside.

"You don't think she's chickened out, do you?" Nick whispered to Patricia once they were inside.

"No way!"

She proved right, and it was only a few minutes later that Stu and Elisabeth were taking off their shoes at the side of the hall. Elisabeth had arrived with Buzz and Laura.

"She cleaned up pretty well," Nick said.

"Yes, she did. Now stop looking at her," Patricia said, with feigned jealousy.

"No sign of Sally Hawes?" Nick asked, looking around as they moved onto the dance floor.

Patricia shook her head.

"She might show up with someone, but it won't be anyone from the Academy or St. Benedict's."

"Does she ever mention David?"

Patricia gave a smile that some might describe as almost evil.

"She mentions him once in a while," she said. "Sometimes with the sense of a magical memory, and other times, it's with angry humiliation."

She gave an embarrassed smile and giggle.

The band was okay, but not as good as the larger one at the Holly Ball. When they stopped for a break at ten o'clock, the friends gathered at one of the round tables. It was undecorated apart from a white paper covering and a cut-out red paper heart placed in the middle.

The food was similarly low key, but the dance's informality made it popular. It was open to everyone, from freshmen up, though few below their junior year attended.

Buzz, Stu and Nick went to collect the food. It was pizza, chips, cake with pink icing and a paper cup of candy with some "Conversation" hearts, cinnamon hearts, and a Hershey Kiss.

"So, how's it going?" Nick asked Stu.

"Must be going okay," he said. "She hasn't cried yet."

"She looks great," Buzz said. "Doesn't dance badly, either."

Stu smiled but said nothing.

Back at the table, it appeared that Stu had spoken too soon, as Elisabeth's cheeks were covered with tears. She smiled through them as Stu arrived and gave her her food.

"I'll be right back," she said, and headed off.

Laura gave a sigh and set off after her.

The boys looked at Patricia for an explanation.

"Isn't she having a good time?" Stu asked.

"Was it something he did?" Buzz asked, helpfully.

Patricia smiled and shook her head.

"She's having a wonderful time," she said. "That's just it: she has trouble coping with happiness."

"Come on!" Buzz exclaimed, but Stu recognized the truth of what she said.

"We got a little insight into some of the sadness," Patricia said.

"I thought that was mostly her mother who suffered," Buzz said.

"Elizabeth's father, uncle and one of her mother's good friends – all dead within a few years," Patricia said. "Combined with living on their own in the boonies, can't have made it easier."

Laura and Elisabeth returned and they started eating.

"Mmm! Nothing like cold pizza and warm Coke!" Buzz said.

They all laughed, but a moment later, Stu saw that Elisabeth's tears had re-started. He didn't blame Buzz, as he could have just as easily said it himself. Apart from passing her a spare napkin, Stu made no mention of it.

"That first half went really fast," he said.

"It was good, and good to see so many here," Laura agreed.

"For someone who says they haven't been to any dances, you dance well," Stu said quietly to Elisabeth.

"I dance in my bedroom," she said.

"Most girls do, but you must have been watching *American Bandstand*, too, to know the moves," he said.

Elisabeth smiled, but said nothing.

When they finished the pizza and started on the candy, Buzz began reading the messages on the hearts.

"I don't think these have changed for years," Patricia said.

"Probably not for over a century," Buzz said. "They started making these before the Civil War."

"Really?"

"Yep. They were invented by the brother of the guy who invented NECCO Wafers," he said.

"You are so full of it, Buzz!" Laura exclaimed, laughing.

"It's *true*!" he protested. "It's all from Massachusetts, too. Hearts, NECCO Wafers and Valentines."

"We're not buying it, Buzz."

The girls went to prepare for the next round.

"Don't you hate being right?" Nick asked, with a laugh.

"It is true – "

"We *know*," Stu said. "The only person who doesn't know is you – when you're being teased."

"Really?"

"Not all girls are dumb, Buzz."

They finished their Cokes.

"Does Elisabeth talk to you?" Nick asked Stu.

"Not really," he said. "Of course, I've hardly seen her."

"Did you talk at Sillitoe's?"

"*I* did. She didn't say much."

"And at her house?"

"I figured she was embarrassed by all the attention," he replied.

"Do you know where she's going to college?"

He shook his head.

"I don't even know *if* she's going to college."

"Is her mystery part of the attraction?"

Stu put up his hands.

"Possibly," he said. "For whatever reason, she asked me to the first dance she's ever gone to, and she seems to like me. So far, she's been easy company – "

"Apart from the crying," Buzz interrupted.

Stu nodded his head.

"I do wish I knew what was going on," he said.

The girls arrived back at the table as the band took the stage again and began to tune and test the mikes and amplifiers.

The music started and they went onto the dance floor.

Patricia nudged Nick and nodded towards Stu and Elisabeth. She had taken his hand and looked perfectly content.

ꕤ

Nick telephoned Patricia Sunday afternoon to thank her for inviting him.

"It went well, didn't it?" she said. "I phoned some friends who were on the dance committee after lunch, and they said they reckoned it was the best Valentine's Dance so far. More people were there than ever before."

"At least there was no more drama," Nick said.

"Not that we saw, but I expect there were tears before bedtime.

"I hope he has the sense to call her or meet her to let her know he had a good time," she continued. "It would be terrible if she was just left hanging."

"I think Stu knows he's dealing with someone special – different. Does he even have a phone number for her?"

Patricia laughed.

"Oh, yes! We made sure of that!"

ꕤ

When Nick saw Stu Monday at the bus stop, he was still in a buoyant mood.

"Good dance, wasn't it?" Nick opened.

Stu gave him a big smile.

"It was a good evening," he said. "I called her yesterday and we talked for nearly an hour."

"Both of you, or just you?"

"Both of us. She opened up a bit more. You know she's been accepted at both Wellesley and Smith! I didn't realize she was *that* brainy. It's rather scary."

"I guess that's why she likes you and Buzz," Nick said. "She can feel even smarter."

"At the end of the dance, I asked her to the St. Benedict's Prom," he said.

"Let me guess: she burst into tears."

"Well, yes," he said. "But she threw her arms around me – she's very strong, nearly knocked me over because I wasn't expecting that reaction."

"But did she say, 'Yes'? That's the real issue," Nick laughed.

"Yes, she said yes, and clung to me the rest of the evening."

"Way to go!"

"When are you seeing her again?" Nick asked.

"I thought I'd go over Saturday afternoon," he said. "There's supposed to be a load of snow Saturday night."

☙

Stu did visit Elisabeth at her home, and she was delighted with the attention. He continued to visit and take her out, either in a group, or on their own. As the weather improved, they walked and explored further afield, shopping, hiking, and studying in the sun.

In early May, after getting off the bus, Stu saw Nick and made the "Let's go to Earnie's Kitchen" gesture, and over iced-tea, Stu brought Nick fully up-to-date.

"How are things going?" Nick asked.

"I wish I knew."

He detailed dates, roamings and other activities he and Elisabeth shared.

"But you know, she still cries every time. She can't – or won't – tell me why, but every damn time!"

"Does she hate saying goodbye that much?"

Stu smiled.

"Now, I could understand that!" he cracked, "but sometimes she cries when I arrive."

"I can see how that might put you off."

"I'm serious, Nick. I've never known anything like it," he said. "At least on the plus side, if it is when I arrive, I talk to her mother while Elisabeth cleans up. She's actually quite an impressive lady."

"Does she say anything about the crying?"

"Nothing. It's as though she doesn't see it," he said, sounded puzzled. "She does keep saying that she's experienced a lot of sadness."

"So, is the prom still on?"

"I guess so. She talks about it, with hints about what she'll wear, or asking how I want her to wear her hair," Stu replied.

"How do you want her to wear her hair?"

"How the hell should I know?" he said, nearing exasperation. "But, somehow, I think she's growing a bit cooler."

"You sure it's not you who's having a drop in temperature?" Nick asked.

"No," he smiled. "I still think she's great – a bit odd – but great."

"Well, I guess that's what matters," Nick said.

"You don't think I should *do* something?"

"Like what?"

ℰ𝒪

A few weeks later, on a Saturday afternoon, Stu and Buzz drove out to the Westerns'. Elisabeth had gone into Royalston to pick up food for the rest of the weekend, but her mother expected her home soon.

They sat on the front porch and chatted easily. Mrs. Western was used to Stu now, and conversation was easy, with Mrs. Western laughing at nearly everything he said.

While more serious, in his conversation Buzz was careful not to pry into their lives, but tried to finesse the occasional nugget of information. What had gradually emerged was how hard both of them had taken the death of Mr. Western. Knowing one or two other school friends who had lost a parent, he had some idea of how traumatic it was.

On this particular afternoon, they discussed the coming prom. Mrs. Western gave nothing away about Elisabeth's plans, but asked about the format, theme, number of couples, and other details.

While they were talking, Elisabeth drove up.

Stu went to the car to meet her and helped her into the house with the shopping bags.

"I can't stay long, but I wanted to see you and say hi," he said.

"You had time for my mother," she said, then laughed. "You could have called and saved yourself the trip."

"I wanted to surprise you," he said, sensing the chill.

She didn't reply until she had loaded things into the refrigerator. She then turned to him, smiled and played with his shirt buttons.

"Yes, that was nice," she said, but Stu wondered if it was.

They went onto the porch to rejoin her mother and Buzz.

"Didn't you offer these guys a drink?" she asked.

"Of course, she did," Buzz said, jumping to Mrs. Western's defense. "The thing is, we can't stay, we're on our way to pick up a hedge trimmer and other garden stuff from my uncle in Athol. Stu persuaded me to make the dogleg to come here."

He looked at his watch and made a face.

Elisabeth sat down but didn't seem to relax.

"Are you okay?" Stu asked.

She smiled.

"Just busy. Term papers," she said. "Two due next week."

Both boys nodded sympathetically.

"We had two this week and one next week," Buzz said. "Teachers like to crack the whip right up until the last minute."

Mrs. Western laughed.

"Come on, Romeo," Buzz said. "We've got to get going."

He and Mrs. Western began walking to the car while Stu and Elisabeth stood close and whispered to each other.

"You *are* okay?"

"Just a little stressed," she said.

"Send a smoke signal if you need anything," he said.

She turned away and went into the house.

The two said goodbye to Mrs. Western who was still laughing at something Buzz had said.

Before getting into the car, Stu looked up at the house and waved to Elisabeth who was watching from a window. Mrs. Western waved to them as Buzz turned the car around (in about eight turns).

"Still good?" Buzz asked.

"I hope so," Stu replied. "This was the first time I've seen her that she didn't cry.

"I thought you'd be relieved."

"So did I."

Elisabeth continued to watch from her window as her mother waved to the car as it headed down the drive, leaving a cloud of dust behind. When Mrs. Western turned back to the house, she was still smiling. She looked up and saw Elisabeth and waved.

As she watched, something stirred that Elisabeth had not felt in a long time.

Then, the wave of weeping began, and she even sobbed as she watched her mother enter the house. She gave one final wave at the empty drive before turning from the window.

She was now certain what she must do.

The Diogenes Club

The Diogenes Club

The Membership Committee
are pleased to announce that
you have been elected to

FULL FELLOWSHIP
of
THE DIOGENES CLUB

It came in a white, unmarked envelope with the postmark of a small town in the Home Counties. I read the formal card several times, wondering what it was all about.

I had not applied for membership, and I thought it curious that the announcement had not mentioned me by name – if, indeed, it was meant for me. The only Diogenes Club I had heard of was that rather mysterious one to which Sherlock Holmes' brother belonged.

The thought that the announcement was some clever, albeit expensive, advertising gimmick crossed my mind.

I placed the card on my mantel in the hope that I might hear from them again and learn more.

The idea of an advertisement made the most sense. I was no one special. I was ordinary, nearly invisible. I went to work, paid my bills, and kept to myself.

A fortnight later, I heard from them again, but I did not learn more.

This time, I received a short, handwritten letter which mentioned the announcement and requested a reply, giving my acceptance. The address was little help: "The Diogenes Club, Nr. Little Goring, Hertfordshire."

Writing back was difficult. I wanted to politely acknowledge receipt of the announcement and the letter, but at the same time indicate my uncertainty.

A fortnight after writing, I received another letter assuring me that there had been no mistake, and if I would be ready to travel to the club the following Friday, arrangements were in hand to take me.

I looked around my room and out into the crowded and noisy street below. Lorries, buses, cars and people going in every direction; shouting and being shouted at in four different languages.

If the Diogenes Club were as respectable as its communications, I wouldn't have expected anyone in it to be concerned with residents of my neighbourhood.

Still, a change of scene (and decibel levels) would be welcome.

There was very little difficulty in being ready by Friday. Recently laid off in "the cuts," I had no job to leave, only distant relatives and few possessions. I packed a suitcase and put my nearly worthless cheque book in my pocket and waited.

At precisely the appointed hour, there was a sharp rap on my door. As in second rate films, a liveried chauffeur stood before me and took my shabby suitcase to an awaiting black Daimler. In the past eight months, I had not seen a parking space that big on my whole street, but there was the car, neatly parked before the door.

It was a long journey north, made longer by Friday night traffic. After the strangeness of the car wore off, I began to play with the knobs and buttons by the armrest. One turned on a compartment lamp and I saw an envelope in the pocket before me. My name was on it.

The brief message told me to help myself to the contents of the decanters and humidor. Opening the cabinet, I found a telephone, small television and several magazines.

I read a magazine, had a drink and dozed.

It was eight-thirty when we passed through some gates and proceeded up a long drive of several miles. A house came into view. Large. Georgian. The doorway was lit, and light also peeked through gaps in the curtains in other rooms. In spite of the mystery, it looked welcoming.

Inside, I was immediately met by a tall, distinguished man of about sixty, dressed for dinner.

"So, you decided to join us after all? Good, good."

He shook my hand firmly.

"Tired after the trip? Jackson will take your bags upstairs. You should have just enough time to change. Dinner is at nine. We'll all be there."

Having said this, the man retired through a magnificent double-door and left me alone in the great hall. The furnishings were lush, well-kept, brightly lit. A long stairway wound its way to the upper floors.

"This way, sir," a voice said.

Jackson was there, holding my suitcase.

He led the way up to the second floor and along a carpeted corridor. Putting down the case, he withdrew a key from his pocket, unlocked the door, then gave me the key.

"Your key, sir."

I followed Jackson inside. He switched on the light, illuminating a large, comfortable sitting room. "Clothes are in the wardrobe in the bedroom. There are cupboards and a private bath. I trust you'll be comfortable. If you require anything, the bell's by the fireplace. You may have a drink on your own, or join the others in the drawing room any time before nine."

I looked at my watch. I wouldn't have time to explore just yet. I found a dinner jacket, shirt and accessories where Jackson had told me. They were the correct size. I washed and dressed quickly, only just making it downstairs as the other members were crossing the hall to the dining room.

Jackson had changed from chauffeur to butler and stood at the entrance to the dining room. "The third place on the left is yours, sir."

I stood by "my place" and waited for everyone to assemble, which they did in silence. The man who had met me at the door took the chair at the head of the table. The chair at the opposite end was set, but vacant.

In the silence, he recited a Latin grace of the Oxbridge variety and we sat down.

Immediately, conversation began, as if it had never been interrupted, in the middle of sentences and discussions. I could hear a wide range of topics as I cast an eye along the table: politics, philosophy, physics, astronomy, art and horses.

I said nothing, and was not spoken to, though a complete meal was served. There were twelve men at the table, each with three crystal glasses and individual salt and pepper sets.

Following the pudding, a yellow chartreuse soufflé, the man at the head of the table rose. "Gentlemen. We must welcome our new member."

"Hear, hear!"

They rose, and I was toasted. Then, the gentleman

continued.

"We must have some introductions. I am Bunthorne, President of the Diogenes Club. On my left, and proceeding clockwise are Drago, Milcrist, Dr Sedgwick, Putman, Major Dutton, Hall, Brown, Hudson, Dr Norton and Barnes. We are the Diogenes Club. I think you'll find us easy enough to get along with."

At this point, Jackson placed a decanter of port before Bunthorne, who poured himself a healthy glass and passed it before he resumed.

"Our rules are simple and few. Breakfast's from eight to nine-thirty. Luncheon from one to two-thirty. Tea at five in the conservatory and drinks from eight o'clock. Dinner is always at nine. Of course, you may have meals brought to your room at any time, or should you be adventuresome, Jackson can show you the kitchens.

"You'll learn of the amenities of the club from all of us. Should you choose to speak to us. No guests are ever allowed into this building, but there are rooms at the pavilion where you may entertain.

"There is never any talking in the library.

"That should cover everything. Shall we adjourn to the drawing room? Bring your glass." We gathered before the fireplace and Bunthorne raised his glass.

"Diogenes."

"Diogenes!"

The painting above the fireplace was a classical figure

and looked like an unknown Rembrandt. I later found no member willing to speculate on the artist or origins of the picture.

We settled ourselves in comfortable chairs. No one seemed particularly concerned who sat where. I was next to an amiable gentleman of about fifty.

"Glad you could make it," he said. "Major Dutton, in case you didn't get all the names."

"Thank you. I'm – I'm rather bewildered. I don't understand any of this, I'm afraid."

"No matter. You'll get used to it. You'll find most of us tolerable. When we're out of sorts, we stay in our rooms, or in the library, or somewhere else at any rate."

"May I ask how I was chosen for membership."

"Simplest thing, my boy. Your name was proposed, seconded and voted upon."

"But I don't know anyone here."

"Does it matter? We know a great deal about you."

He sipped his port.

"Was everyone there for dinner?"

"Oh, yes," the major replied. "That was all of us."

"What about – "

"Ah! The empty place. For Diogenes, of course!"

He gave an easy laugh.

"Hopefully, we're all honest men; he may find us one day."

I said nothing, but must have looked bewildered.

"Don't worry. Things will sort themselves out."

"It's a grand club," I began, tentatively. "I'm a little anxious about the, how shall I say it, terms of membership."

"Basically, it's as Bunthorne said. The only other rules are those of common decency: refold the *Times* properly and that sort of thing."

"I really meant financial arrangements, I'm afraid."

"Money? Never touch the stuff, personally. No need. Still, if you need any, Drago's the man to see. Anything over a thousand he likes a day's notice for, but usually there's no difficulty."

"I see."

I didn't see.

"You must excuse me now. I have a standing billiards game with Dr Sedgwick. I'll turn you over to Hudson, here."

The major left with a friendly wave, and Hudson took his seat.

Hudson was a much younger man, in his forties, I thought. I guessed him to be the member nearest my own age. He had a public school and Oxbridge manner, but there was no way to deduce this beyond the impression he gave.

"D'you play golf?" he asked.

"Badly."

"Good. I'm dreadful, too. Top handicap. Perhaps we

can teach ourselves the game."

The rolling of dice and the clicking of backgammon discs came from the corner of the room. The air was scented with a fine Havana aroma. A Mozart piano concerto played quietly on an unseen system.

"I understand all the members are here tonight," I said. "How often do you all get together?"

"I beg your pardon."

"How often does the club meet like this?"

"My dear fellow," Hudson exclaimed with surprise, "the club always meets like this. We live here – and so do you, now. Of course, people come and go on holiday every now and then; or sometimes to the theatre, or a weekend in London, but usually everyone stays pretty close to home."

"You live here; permanently?"

"Of course."

"What about your – "

Some how the word didn't seem to fit to be uttered here.

" – your work?"

"Work? Hasn't' Bunthorne told you anything?"

"Only what you heard at dinner tonight."

I told him about the announcements and letters.

"I suppose that's right. I hardly remember coming here myself. It must have been twelve or fourteen years ago. I barely remember not being here. You're the first member since then. Quite an occasion, really. Have some more port."

From that point, Hudson spoke a monologue about a variety of subjects, mostly his varied interests, but not a word about the Diogenes Club. He was an interesting man and our interests were similar.

Shortly after ten-thirty, I felt tired (and confused) and after saying good night to the remaining members in the drawing room, retired upstairs.

After finding the way back to my room, I noticed that the key I withdrew from my pocket was silver.

In my room, I changed from the dinner jacket and relaxed in the chair in the sitting room – *my* sitting room. I had a large suite, the sitting room was easily twenty feet long, with high ceilings and a fireplace. The bedroom was slightly smaller, but spaciously arranged. Jackson apparently had been in during the evening as the bed was turned down and the fires were lit. Other furniture included end tables, a small Chesterfield, a large desk, book shelves, (partially filled) and several side chairs. I also had ample cupboard space and a large bathroom. It was thoroughly comfortable.

I had no business in such surroundings. In my life, there was nothing to warrant this, I reflected. What I had been, I ceased to be as soon as I stepped into the Diogenes Club. I had no particular family connections; my contact with important or influential people was brief and shallow. One does not make powerful friends in jobs like I had.

You see, there were two problems to solve: What was the Diogenes Club, and why was I now a part of it? The only remotely notable thing I had done was to write a few articles for work that had been published in a trade magazine.

I was not a man of great faith; never one to go to the wall for principle, but I was not one to be used, either. A fitting epitaph? Or just one word: Mediocrity. Partially educated, partially cultured, partially bluff – just an average late twentieth century man.

Trying to puzzle it out would lead nowhere, I decided. I did not yet have enough evidence. I rose from my chair and poured a drink from the tantalus by the desk.

The next step in the labyrinth was now that I had arrived, what was expected of me? My instincts kept asking questions, while my indolent side kept telling me not to look for trouble.

I reviewed the evening carefully, step by step, conversation by conversation. Only one thing struck me as unusual – that there was nothing unusual about anyone there.

My dreams that night were the victim of an overactive imagination that had read too much Alistair MacLean.

In the morning, I went downstairs and was shown the breakfast room. The hearty breakfast was set out on the sideboard. Messrs Brown, Hall and Barnes were there, and Dr Sedgwick.

"Do the others not come down?" I asked Barnes.

"Bunthorne and Drago always have something in their rooms. There are several who never breakfast, and even one or two who prefer to make their own. It rather depends what they plan to do that day."

What did anyone in the Diogenes Club do? I wondered.

"As this is my first morning, perhaps you could suggest how I might best spend it."

I was irritated that my conversation was beginning to sound like a Victorian novel. ("After taking breakfast, a habit seldom broken by the older members of the Diogenes Club, it was time to plan the day; that curious process at which considerable time is spent to very little purpose.")

"My dear chap," Barnes began, "I would never presume to tell you what to do here. It's against all the rules. However, you might have a look through the house, see our library, the games room and take a long walk in the grounds. There are five hundred acres. You've been told about the golf course; there are also stables. Help yourself to a good horse if you like. I dare say you'll find enough to occupy your time. Do you play bridge?"

"Badly."

I'd said the same about golf recently, too.

"Well, when you get better at it, we'll play."

He gulped the last of his coffee and excused himself. I finished breakfast and went to the library in the hopes of inheriting a newspaper from someone. Five men were already behind their papers and I looked about for another. My eyes fell on the large mahogany table. Five papers lay there, each with a name neatly written in the corner. My name was on one.

Bunthorne and Drago, no doubt, had theirs upstairs. The luxury of not having to hurry through a paper, and not to be interrupted once, is not to be underrated. Indeed, I cannot recall six men in a single room ever making less noise.

But, my experience is common, I had had no previous glimpse into such serenity before. Nonetheless, I was anxious to get outside once I had finished the paper. I took a coat from my room (the bed was made and the room had been tidied by unseen hands) and began to explore.

It was a brisk November morning. Leaves still clung to a few persistent oaks, and bright blue patches fought off the advancing grey clouds. The grass shivered in the chill breeze. I walked past the golf course and soon sensed that the stables were near. No one was about, but the heads of several horses peering from their stalls seemed to indicate that someone was expected shortly.

Beyond the stables, barn and paddock, the countryside opened into broad fields and pastures. Some were cultivated while others lay fallow and had begun to merge into the wood beyond. I walked for nearly an hour, encountering no one, nor any sign of anyone. The woods were deep and cold. It was a vague sort of path I followed. In about twenty minutes, it brought me to the edge of a small lake.

It was peaceful and undisturbed.

I am one who finds solitude in a large city lonely, but not solitude in nature; but that day, by the edge of the lake, it was a feeling of loneliness which came over me, like a child in his first week at school.

Things were strange. I didn't know the people I was living with; I didn't know how I came to be there, or why. I didn't know if I was free to leave. Would someone stop me from passing through the gates?

That thought frightened me so much I was afraid to find the answer.

I thought of my rooms back in London. Would anyone miss me? How long would it take before the landlord made inquiries? Or, would the Diogenes Club take care of things there, too?

Following the water's edge all the way round, I lost myself eventually in nature and forgot all about the

Diogenes Club.

It was mid-afternoon when I returned to the club. I had missed lunch but would be able to have tea shortly. I went to my rooms for a brief rest and saw that a silver plate had been fixed to my door, engraved with my name.

ca

Tea was a friendly affair. I chatted to Barnes and Hudson who had supposed me to be out exploring.

"Take a horse next time," said Barnes. "It'll get you further – and back in time for lunch."

I saw Bunthorne.

"Is it possible," I began, "to go back to London shortly?"

"Certainly. What for?"

"Just to collect some things from my flat."

"No need, my boy. They should be here in a few days. The removal firm begins Monday. Everything should be here by Wednesday."

I felt trapped. I couldn't believe the organisation.

"I would still like to go to London," I said.

"Can't see why, but speak to Jackson. He will arrange a car for you. Will you want a driver as well? Just tell him. And see Drago if you want some money. He does like a few days' notice for anything over a thousand."

After those brief words with Bunthorne, Hudson and I played backgammon until it was time to change for dinner.

Dinner was just as it had been the night before.

ꙮ

Several days later, my belongings were delivered from London. Those things I did not have immediate use for were stored in a personal box room in the attics.

Seeing all the possessions of my life neatly boxed and stored in the attic of the Diogenes Club was like hearing the screws turn on my own coffin. The feeling of being trapped, which had hitherto only fluttered across my mind, now felt like a pall. All I ever had to show for in the world was now in this building, forever beyond the ordinary day to day life of which I had once been a part.

My fellow members were always very pleasant. Except during after dinner discussions, I never heard anyone raise a voice. I never sensed dislike, or intolerance. All the gentlemen were exceedingly cordial. I never felt the "junior member" or the "new boy," nor have I reason to believe that I was ever considered one. But in spite of the camaraderie and nearly limitless opportunity to pursue my interests, I felt, more and more, that I must know whether I was being held prisoner or not.

Objectively, it must look an easy problem: send for a car and drive away. But from my own, limited, perspective, it was not that simple. Consider: if I did get away, would I be able to return? Would I be as genially treated upon my return? And, would I be able to get away again?

Supposing that I could just drive away, where would I go? If I requested a substantial sum from Drago and did a bunk, would I be pursued? Prosecuted? Eliminated?

Knowing that delay could be fatal, I delayed.

A fortnight passed in splendid comfort and company before I requested that Jackson hire a car for me. Drago gave me five hundred pounds.

It was exhilarating, sitting behind the wheel of the rented Scimitar and revving the engine before the door to the Diogenes Club. Even there, I felt free.

With self-satisfied assuredness, I put the machine into gear and shot down the drive. The gates were open and I chased through them.

Without the slightest idea of where I was or where I was going, I raced down the country lanes. The feel of the snug seat and the response of the car gave more pleasure and excitement than I had ever experienced driving.

I passed through several small villages; beautiful, well-kept little places of timbered buildings and northern stone. I drove as fast as I dared for nearly an hour before stopping in one of them.

The bar at the Black Swan was only partially full. I ordered a ploughman's with my pint and revelled in my freedom.

The bar filled with people, smoke and noise. I loved

it. For about ten minutes; then left.

A walk through the village turned up nothing of particular interest: a shop of over-priced antiques; a shop of second-hand books – that resembled nothing more than the contents of a dull vicar's library – and a small news agent's and grocery.

A double-decker Green Line choked into the village and dropped off an over-weight woman and two children sucking lollies. One child dropped his and it stuck in the gutter. He howled. The woman struck him and told him to shut up, and he howled the louder.

It was not for this scene that I hired a new Scimitar and had drawn five hundred pounds.

Back in the car, I continued along the road, taking only right hand turnings. The day had grown cloudy and would surely rain before long. I was driving at a moderate speed and was feeling a little bored.

I was neither surprised nor disappointed to see the gates of the Diogenes Club.

ꟸ

At dinner, no one was particularly interested to know where I had been or what I had done. The ones who knew I had gone out politely asked if I had had a good drive and if I had gone anywhere in particular.

I returned £ 491.50 to Drago.

In the days that followed, I found my notebooks and resumed work on a short story that I had begun a decade earlier after the publication of my articles for work. I enjoyed writing and, after the business articles were published, thought I'd try my hand at a short story. I had the idea, but not the confidence or drive to finish it. Perhaps now I could.

One thing I did not have was an electronic typewriter. Just as a child is convinced that he will do something better with the best gear, I had used the idea as an incentive to write.

"Shall we order you one, or would you like to pick out your own?" Bunthorne asked.

"I know what I want."

I gave him the details and within two days, I was seated before it at my desk.

I wrote a short story and addressed it to a magazine. Instead of taking it to the letter-box myself, I went to the bell-pull by the fireplace and rang for Jackson. I had never used it before, but, proud of my efforts, I did so then.

"Please see that this is posted at the earliest opportunity, Jackson," I said.

Everything was posted at the earliest opportunity; efficiency was a cardinal rule of the Diogenes Club.

My resolution to post a story each fortnight became a story each month, then each quarter.

☙

I have felt most contented here now for the past eight

years. After that single drive in the country, I have never again felt trapped, nor the need for further excursions.

Only once since then did a nasty feeling creep over me. I had had a restless night with dreadful dreams. I woke up convinced that the Diogenes Club was some carefully run asylum, with Bunthorne the director.

I remained in my room after that for three days and had my meals sent up to me. I thought I might force the doctor's hand and someone would visit my room to find out what had brought about the radical change of habit.

No one came.

When I resumed my normal routine, no one commented.

It may be an asylum, but did that really change anything? The meals, the members, the grounds, the food and my typewriter and books were all here.

Knowing that I was insane or under treatment would change nothing except my perception of myself. Were these elegant surroundings real, or illusions of my madness?

Eventually, I concluded that it didn't matter.

So, here's another little story.

I shall ring for Jackson to post it at the earliest opportunity.

Sugaring Up

Sugaring Up

Sadie Baker loved winter. She always had, and that was a good thing because she lived in New Hampshire where winter took up much of the year. She'd loved winter from when she was a little girl and played and sledded in the white snow, then thawed out with hot chocolate by the log fire.

It had been a happy childhood and, even then, she had few wishes apart from that things could continue for as long as possible.

Hickman's Falls wasn't an exciting place fifty years ago, and it was even less exciting forty years later. One reason was that there as a good deal less of it now. The general store had closed in her parents' time, replaced for a while by a 7-Eleven. Now that was gone, and to do any shopping, you had to go to Colebrook Falls or Stewartstown. They were hardly exciting places, but they were metropolises compared to Hickman's Falls.

Sadie's family, like most of the others in that part of the world, had a farm. They ran it mostly from habit. They had some ducks and chickens, a few goats and several acres of corn, or wheat, or peas and beans. There were the remnants of an apple orchard with the odd pear tree.

Most of the trees were too old to produce much, but half a dozen produced edible apples, some of which were very good. The rest of the trees were destined for firewood. All these decades later, and they'd still be felled and an apple log would be added to the fire.

There were woods, too. They were on the other side of Route 3, but it was an easy walk. There's not much traffic on the road today, and almost nothing on it when she was growing up. Still, the county kept it plowed and sanded so life could go on regardless of the weather.

Hickman's Falls used to have a small furniture factory, a machine shop and depot where fruit and vegetables were boxed and shipped. Amos and Bart Todd ran a small garage, too. They sold gas but their main business was keeping the ancient cars, trucks and tractors working. They were surprisingly skilled and when parts for the old vehicles became impossible to get – or just too expensive – they'd make them. As a result, Bart split his time between the machine shop and the garage.

As an example, a local resident with a relatively new car had had it serviced at the dealership in St. Johnsbury where the "skilled automotive technician" had cross-threaded the bung in the sump resulting in a slow drip that stained the owner's driveway and garage.

A call to the dealership to complain received a short, "That's not something our technicians would do." Amos and Bart, drained the oil, removed the sump, cleaned it out, filled it with sand, re-drilled and threaded the hole to one millimeter larger than standard, then machined a new bung, flushed out the sand, refitted the sump and put in new oil.

The whole bill came to fifty bucks, thirty of which was for the replacement oil. How they made a living, few people knew, but they retired when they were about seventy, leaving the village without a gas station or a place for tractor repairs.

Sadie could just about remember trains running through Hickman's Falls. There was a small freight depot with a siding off the single-track line. It was a branch of the Maine Central that ran from North Stratford in New Hampshire, to Beecher's Falls, Vermont.

Passenger services had stopped before Sadie was born, but her parents and neighbors used to tell stories that while Hickman's Falls had no station (the nearest being Canaan or Colebrook), all anyone had to do was stand near the siding junction and wave and the train would stop to pick them up.

The train might make a dozen or more unscheduled stops along its route. Often farmers would load milk churns, baskets of fruit or vegetables into the baggage car and ride with it to their destination. Although there might be only a dozen people on the train at any one time, more than a hundred people may have boarded and departed along its thirty mile route.

There had been a coffee shop on Route 3. About all it did was serve coffee, but a number of locals supplied it with pies (apple, blueberry or pumpkin depending on the season), doughnuts, and bottles of maple syrup to sell. Others made a few sandwiches each day. Anything that was unsold was collected by a charity in Canaan which distributed it, mostly to unemployed mill workers and their families.

Canaan was where Sadie had gone to Mascoma Valley Regional High School and met Boyd Allen who would become her husband.

He had played football for "The Royals" and was personable, if quiet. Sadie herself was also quiet. Neither of them was an exceptional student, and it was in an "extra help" class that they got to know each other.

Boyd lived on a farm about halfway between Canaan and Hickman's Falls. He had two older brothers and two sisters, one older, one younger. His position in the family put him under pressure, and this was the subject of their first serious conversation.

"What are you going to do when you graduate?" Sadie asked him, while waiting to be collected.

Boyd didn't answer immediately and Sadie wondered if it was embarrassment or something else.

"I don't know," he eventually replied, his voice very quiet.

She waited to see if anything further would follow.

"I've been thinking of little else," he said. "All summer while I was working in the warehouse, all I could think was, 'I don't want to do this for the rest of my life,' but I never thought of anything else.

"I could go into the army or navy," he added.

"What about the farm?" she asked. "I thought you loved farming."

"I do, but I'm the third son," he replied. "Jeb will inherit the farm and, if something happens to him, it will go to Burt."

Sadie considered this and continued to think.

Boyd wasn't bad looking. He liked farming, while not an academic firework, he worked hard and, he was a football and ice hockey player.

They saw each other off and on until graduation, mostly at school events or with friends, but they would occasionally go to the movies or to someplace to eat further afield. Neither of them had much money, but they didn't mind spending it on each other.

"Why don't you work for your brother?" she asked one evening.

Boyd made a face.

"I'd like to be more than just a hired hand," he said, but without resentment. "The day will come when Jeb wants the house to himself and a family. I don't mind working for him until then, but none of the farms around here make much money."

That was true. Every year, the costs went up and the food buyers and distributors wanted to pay less.

It was something that everyone talked about. Some concluded that selling up and moving was the best answer.

"I hope my folks don't sell up," Sadie had said, about a year after they'd graduated. "I'd hope that they would buy more land from those who are leaving."

"What would you do with more land?" Boyd asked.

Boyd was now working for his parents with his brothers, and Sadie and her mother made pies, sandwiches and cakes. Depending on the season, they would also sell fruit and vegetables.

Sadie would make deliveries up and down Route 3, sometimes going into Beecher's Falls where there were a few good customers. She'd try to time things so she could meet Boyd for lunch once or twice a week.

"What would you do with all that land?" Boyd asked.

"You know our land on the river has two big bends?"

"Yeah, it looks like a backwards three," he replied.

"Well, that gives us more land along the river," Sadie resumed. "We farm it a little, but it's awkward to plow. I thought it might make a good campsite. Plant some more trees, build some nice, simple cabins and rent them to fishermen and kayakers."

Boyd considered this.

"Not a bad idea," he said, obviously thinking about it carefully. "Some picnic tables – and you could sell them some food. Maybe even lay on a barbecue once a week, or a big family style meal."

"Like a pig roast," Sadie said, enthusiastically.

Boyd thought some more.

"How much maple syrup do you make?" he asked.

"Not a lot. We usually just make it for ourselves," she said. "The big farms dominate the market. All the regulations are a pain, too."

"Yes, but once you've got the standards, you've got them," Boyd argued. "So how many gallons?"

"Only about ten."

"That's eighty pints."

"We mostly sell by half-pints."

Boyd thought.

"We do about forty gallons."

"You've got more woods," Sadie said.

"Well, you're going to buy up all that land from the leavers!" he retorted, and they both laughed.

They didn't discuss it any further that day, but both of them nurtured their ideas.

ᘓ

In the years after graduation, they continued to see each other more and more regularly. They'd drop by each other's farms and help each other for a few hours, particularly on the weekends.

When the spring came, Boyd came by to help Sadie tap the maples. There was still a lot of snow, and it was fun to see their footsteps going to each tree. It wasn't hard work, it just took time. They drove into the woods as far as they could get the truck, which wasn't more than about a quarter mile, and began work. After a few trees, they divided the work so they could do it quickly.

When they finished for the day, Sadie fell over backwards into the soft snow.

Boyd was alarmed but as he rushed towards her, she started moving her arms and legs, making a snow angel. He laughed and lay down near her and did the same.

"I've loved doing this for as long as I can remember," she said, and laughed.

While down in the snow, they took the opportunity to roll around, not making any shapes in particular.

Back at the house, Mrs. Baker made some hot chocolate and had just placed it on the table when Sadie ran out of the house.

Again, Boyd was surprised by her sudden escape and stood to follow, but she quickly returned with two bowls of packed snow which she put on the table.

Mrs. Baker caught on and placed two spoons at their places while Sadie put a pint bottle of maple syrup on the table.

Boyd laughed and looked relieved.

Sadie began pouring the syrup liberally over her snow, and Boyd followed suit.

"I know this is called a lot of different things," Sadie began, "but we've always called it 'Sugaring up'."

"That's what my family called it," her mother said. "Your father's family called it 'Maple toffee,' but they rolled it up on a stick."

The two women looked at Boyd.

"My father calls it 'Maple snow' but my mother calls it 'Sugaring Up', too."

"And what do you call it, Boyd?" Mrs. Warner asked.

"I'll call it whatever Sadie wants me to."

☙

Understandings were given and after a few years of working for their respective parents, Sadie married Boyd Allen. Boyd worked on the Baker farm.

Sadie worked on her plans for a campsite and also for acquiring more land so that they could make a larger contribution to the maple syrup business on the Allen's farm.

That part had gone well. Boyd was on good terms with his brother Jeb, and Sadie got on well enough with Jeb's wife, Barbara. If Sadie thought her own ambitions were modest, Barbara lowered the bar considerably with her lack of ambition or vision.

Boyd was content to work and leave the decisions to Sadie and her father. It was more their farm than his, he believed. He would, however, not be afraid to object if he thought something was a really bad idea.

He was against borrowing money, for one thing. He'd work like a dog to avoid it.

"I know it will slow things down a year or two, but we won't owe anyone anything, and that's important," he argued, and eventually Sadie and her father listened.

Their vision for the camp site was to keep it small, affordable for them and the campers, but keep the standards high.

They planted trees and set out areas for tents and five cabins. People could feel private.

What this meant was that in addition to general farming, Boyd did a lot of digging. He rented equipment when he had the money and dug trenches for the water and electricity entrances for the shower and toilet block and the cabins (although they wouldn't be built for another five years – why hire the digger twice?).

He dug the hole for the septic tank and trenches for the septic field.

At each stage, the family would revisit the plans and discuss the next move. They were good discussions, but, in the end, a decision was made and everyone was still speaking.

During the winter, more plans were made. Once the snow came, there was little to do except care for the animals, sharpen tools, clear out storage buildings, order seed, plants, fertilizer, service the cars, truck and tractors, and prepare for the maple syrup season.

Sadie and her mother made quilts. These sold for high prices and while labor intensive, it was enjoyable work for several hours each day. They could make one a month each in addition to the sandwich, pie and cake making.

One day, Sadie went out to the barn where Boyd was checking the dozens of tapered tin syrup pails. Sadie found an old wooden box and took it to the workbench and stood next to him.

"I'll clean the spiles," she said, taking half a dozen out of the box. There were hundreds of them.

The spiles were used to tap the maple trees. There were dozens of different designs bought over the years, and they were made from different materials: cast iron, aluminum and, the newest, stainless steel.

"There's some steel wool over there," he said, indicating another box.

Only the iron ones needed a brush with the steel wool. They'd all be boiled in water and the cast iron ones would get a light rust removal treatment. The sap would be boiled, so there was no real danger, but it was good practice.

Sadie also inspected the ends that would go into the tree. Nowadays, Boyd had a battery powered drill to cut the holes to set the spiles, but some of the older designs still had a sharp piece that would ensure a good, tight fit. On these old ones, the end looked like a fountain pen nib: curved and pointed. They also had a flat drip end that could take a good whack with the club hammer.

The newer ones had an open-topped drip end so setting the spile had to be done more carefully by hitting the pail-holder.

Sadie picked up a steel file and began filing the sharp ends of the old spiles.

"Jeb said some land is coming up for sale down this way," Boyd said.

"The Warner's land?"

"Yup. Moe Warner came up from Boston to see what could be done," Boyd explained. "The farm hasn't made any money since Old Man Warner died and Moe's mother doesn't want to leave the farm. Selling off land is the only way she'd be able to stay."

"How soon is this going to happen?"

"Not in a hurry," Boyd said, with a chuckle.

"Nothing around here ever happens in a hurry."

"Whoever came up with the term 'Hicktown' must have known Hickman's Falls," he said, and they both laughed.

He wasn't the first to have said it, and he had said it many times before, but it still always got a laugh from those in the area.

"That could be us one day," Sadie observed. "Sad to think of it."

"Then don't, Sadie," he chided. "You're barely twenty-five."

ꕥ

When March came, Boyd and Sadie went out into the woods. They drove up the dirt road as far as they could and parked. They each took ten pails and spiles and set to work.

Boyd would drill a hole (about eight inches from last year's tap, now plugged with a dowel) and move to the next tree. Sadie would tap in the spile, hang the pail and fit the lid, then move to the next tree.

She found the repetition and working in the deep, quiet woods with Boyd romantic and satisfying. Boyd seemed to feel that way, too, as he enjoyed the late snow that began falling as they tapped the last two dozen trees.

When they finished, Sadie fell over backwards and completed her ritual. Though tired, he was in good humor and joined Sadie on the ground and they made angels in the fresh snow.

The marriage had its dark side, too. Two miscarriages and the death of both their fathers within their first decade of married life were each hard to absorb. Boyd's mother died two years after his father.

There was still demand for the quilts that Sadie and her mother made, for the maple syrup, and for the campsite (though campers now wanted wireless broadband connections). The rest of the crops and animals did little more than pay for themselves.

There had been some insurance money on the death of Sadie's father, and they used it to buy the extra land and put the final touches on their campsite. The latter had proved popular with fishermen, as they had hoped, and also with a few painters and writers who came back year after year to spend a few weeks in the cabins.

The fishing had been the one thing that had improved over the decades with reduced pollution. Salmon, trout, striped bass and pike were thriving. The problem was that while the fishermen were more successful, that didn't contribute to Boyd and Sadie's income which remained the same regardless of how the fishermen were doing.

A few years after her father's death, Sadie's mother, having lost her husband and most of her friends, saw no reason to stick around, either, and both farms were now in the hands of another generation.

Sadie and Boyd remained positive over the next years. Things went well, and time passed in its seasonal rhythm. They worked hard, accumulated a little savings, and each year tapped the maples and made snow angels. The sight of a fifty-year-old woman making snow angels isn't attractive, which is why she did it deep in the woods, and anyway, that's not how Boyd saw Sadie as he joined her.

With the improved affluence felt all over the country, there were changes along the upper Connecticut River. Trains no longer ran. New roads took all but local traffic off Route 3. Young people moved to the cities. As a result, the normal markets became more restrictive and, while others prospered, those in the country were squeezed.

The real blow came when Boyd's brother Jeb died suddenly from a heart attack. He was sixty-two.

Like everyone else, Boyd had believed his brothers and himself to be immortal. He mourned his brother every day but was not morbid and continued with his work, and Sadie made daily visits to Joanna, his widow. They had known each other since high school, too, and always got on well.

One night, not long after Jeb was buried, Sadie spoke to Boyd after dinner.

"Have you seen Joanna this week?"

He shook his head.

"I know it's very difficult for you to go without your family there," she continued, gently. "Your nephew Andy is only able to stay a few more days before going back to Boston. He's trying to get her to move."

Boyd continued to stare at his coffee and nodded. Sadie knew he was trying to cope as best he could, but she needed to press on.

"Joanna's not able to run things on her own," she continued. "Andy says even if she stays put, she will have to sell up soon. There's very little money."

Boyd nodded again.

"We depended on Jeb to sell our produce with his," he said. "It kept us both viable."

He looked at her and she saw pain, but also something new: dread.

"Have you got a plan?" she asked.

He was silent for a time, then sighed.

"I'll talk to Joanna tomorrow," he said. "I'll try to get her to move and sell up. We can't afford it, and we couldn't run it if we could. If we're lucky, we've got five years left here ourselves."

Sadie knew this. She worked with Boyd on the accounts, and he hid nothing from her. That's what she loved. Like all men, he hated to show any weakness, but he also believed that both their lives were bound up in the farm – besides, he still considered it hers, although they owned it in common.

When the dominoes fell, they fell quickly.

Boyd and Andy had persuaded Joanna to move and the place went on the market. It was a bigger and better farm than theirs, but Boyd never resented that. He'd been able to work closely with his family his whole life and considered himself blessed.

What Boyd had predicted years before came true: the maple woods were sold to a company that made syrup on an industrial scale while the rest of the farm was sold as lots for houses, light industry and commercial activities. There was talk of a new strip mall, but it never got off the ground as there just wasn't the traffic or population to support it. Instead, a succession of small cafes, specialty shops, hunting and bait and tackle shops rotated regularly through the few buildings that were built over the next decade until they were too run down to attract tenants.

Now in his mid-sixties, Boyd had some more grim news for Sadie. He'd been diagnosed with a heart condition. It was hardly surprising: it's what had killed his father and brother. He was on all sorts of pills and he and Sadie discussed the possibility of an operation – which guaranteed little more than possible survival for another few years – and their future at the farm.

"Do you think we can sell it?" Sadie asked. "The camping is still doing well. You didn't skimp when you built it, and it's paid off."

The camping was not without competition now. Part of the Allen farm had been developed. While compared to the Baker farm, the sites were crammed in, their marketing had been more aggressive, so it was doing well enough for whoever owned it.

"It might sell, but we'd need to decide where to go," he said.

"I'd want to move to a town so you could be near a hospital," she said.

Boyd shook his head.

"No. If I'm going to get sick and die, let me do it here without running up bills," he said. "Even so, there won't be much money."

"Well, if we sold the maple woods, that might work," she said.

He looked at her in disbelief.

"What would you do without those woods?" he asked in amazement.

"Trespass," she replied.

He burst out laughing and leaned over and kissed her.

"Let me think about this because it looks like you will have to be provided for," he said. "There's not much insurance, and while there's no mortgage on the farm, there's very little cash, and I want to ensure that you will be comfortable when I'm gone."

He was a good man, Sadie thought over the next few weeks. He tried hard and he worked hard, but sometimes his thinking wasn't all that creative. He'd come up with the germ of a plan, but Sadie was the one to embellish it and hone it to perfection. Of course, she could never tell Boyd the full details. He wouldn't like it.

Somehow, they survived the next few years and by March, the usual winter chores had been done and it was time to head into the woods again.

It now took them two long days to tap the trees that used to take them just one. Yet, when they finished, they had the same feeling of elation, and Sadie fell easily backwards into the snow laughing, closely followed by Boyd. They laughed all the way home, and once there, Sadie went out in the yard and packed two bowls with snow and set them on the table and fetched spoons and the bottle of syrup.

"Sugaring up," Boyd said.

"Sugaring up," replied Sadie.

"This has been good and I've always – "

Boyd stopped mid-sentence and fell forwards. Sadie screamed his name as she looked at him.

The time had come. She must do this right. Just as she had rehearsed it in her mind, over and over. There would be plenty of time for tears later.

She went to the telephone and dialed 911 but said nothing and let the receiver fall noisily.

She then went into the barn for what she needed. All she had to do was carry out these few simple things and she would be looked after for the rest of her life.

Sadie looked at her dead husband, regarding him no longer as such.

She'd read enough detective stories to know the exact spot. She closed her eyes briefly, took a deep breath and deftly tapped the spile into his skull.

"Goodbye, Boyd," she said, "Thank you."

And then she went outside to make angels in the snow.

The Asher Bar

The Asher Bar

May 2021

I never liked New York much. It's too full of itself for no good reason. In recent years, it has tried to out-do Texas in ego. It doesn't work there, either.

Business is about the only thing that can get me to New York, and that's what got me there this time. It was a conference for the maritime industry. As everyone knows, 2020 was a disastrous year for travel. Dozens of cruise ships were laid up, and now these steel petri dishes needed to be refurbished, sold or scrapped. Freighters and container ships didn't fare much better. Disruption to long-distance supply routes was causing a restructuring of supply chains, the move of manufacturing back to Europe and North America (accelerating the adoption of digital manufacturing), and the consequent consolidation of shipping companies, container shortages and the disposal of surplus vessels.

I work for one of the associated businesses, the necessary, but parasitic world of ship brokers. It was my job to meet with shipping companies to learn of their changing requirements and to help them acquire or, more often, dispose of, ships.

As you might imagine, this was a global business, and we had offices and agents around the world. In 2020, like the rest of the world, most of our business was done by video conferencing, and this is why the conference in New York – the first in two years – was an important event.

When I attended the first of these conferences as a young man, I accompanied my boss, whose position I now hold, and we stayed here at the Beaufort. It became where I always stay.

The Beaufort is a wonderful relic from an earlier age, but it is not easy to tell which. It occupies one of the few remaining mansions of Gilded Age New York. It is hidden in plain sight, tucked at the end of an alley (reminiscent of the Savoy in London) between Park Avenue and Lexington Avenue, almost equidistant from Pennsylvania Station and Grand Central Terminal.

The hotel remains full by word of mouth. It has never advertised and the brass sign by the door simply says, "Beaufort."

The people who come to the Beaufort have come all their lives. Their parents came with their friends, and, in time, their children and *their* friends. It was where they always stayed when in New York.

Admittedly, the hotel was a bit of an anachronism, but it continues to maintain a reasonably high standard in rooms and dining, but it is the service that makes it remarkable. It is unusual for one who has ever stayed there not to be recognized by one or more of the staff.

However, this is not an exclusive hotel – though it isn't always easy to get a room – nor an extravagantly expensive one, and it certainly isn't stuffy. Its atmosphere is akin to that of a long-established country club.

Its ballroom is a perfect mid-size for private functions and weddings that don't get out of hand and, as a result, it is in near-constant use.

I never worked out how many rooms there are at the Beaufort. I suspected, but did not know for certain, that its corridors wandered beyond the original mansion into adjacent buildings.

The final thing to note is the restrained good taste that prevails. Its grand staircase is elegant, but not ostentatious. Ceiling moldings have fine detail but are not fussy, and the remaining murals depict intimate landscapes, not obscure Classical myths.

I was greeted by name at the desk in the foyer. However, along with the usual niceties, Francis, the day manager, said, confidentially:

"You will find the staff on their best behavior," he said. "There are negotiations for the sale of the Beaufort in progress, so please forgive them if they are overly formal."

A worrying development. No one wants his favorite hotel, no matter how tacky, to be changed in any way.

ɞ

For me, the appealing focal point of the hotel is its bar. Quiet and clubby; it is good when entertaining, or reading on one's own with a good drink.

It is universally known as "The Asher Bar," though officially, it is "The Bar at the Beaufort," which is printed on its cocktail napkins, but does not appear elsewhere.

Located on the second floor of the hotel, it is open to the public, but few people other than hotel guests know it is there. It is a civilized haven of comfortable leather chairs, sofas and banquettes, with no piped music or other modern distractions. Indeed, the only concession to the twentieth century was electricity, and there are no concessions to the twenty-first.

Money is not handled in the bar. For those not putting their purchases on their room bill, cash and cards are sent, via pneumatic tube, to the office where change is made and receipts written.

It is easy to miss The Asher Bar completely. The second floor elevator doors open and guests can go to rooms to their left and right. What many do not realize is that the large portrait that confronts them when they step out of the elevator is recessed to create two invisible, doorless entrances to the bar. There are no signs.

The portrait, of course, is an excellent copy of John Singer Sargent's standing portrait of Asher Wertheimer.

Unlike many of Sargent's swagger portraits, old Asher has a friendly, welcoming look. The informality of the pose, with the left hand extended and holding a very convincing cigar, was something that had not been seen in portraiture before. Adding to the informality is the inclusion of Wertheimer's dog. These elements combined to make a subtle statement that a new era was approaching.

When first shown (and later when presented to the National Gallery by Wertheimer), the portrait provoked controversy because, along with its more casual pose, there was considerable anti-Jewish sentiment and the feeling that art dealers were little better than money-lenders.

As none of these things matter in the "modern world," Asher looks quite at home and people respond warmly to his welcoming presence.

I know the portrait well, from its current home at the Tate Gallery as well as at the Beaufort, and my instinct is always to walk up to him and try to shake his hand, though I confine myself to speaking to him.

Sargent obviously felt that way about Asher, too. He painted twelve oil portraits of his family and two watercolor sketches. He is reported to have delighted in the family, enjoyed their sense of fun, and remained friends with the children long after Asher's death in 1918.

What is curious was that Asher is a London art dealer with no significant connections to New York. Why he is in the Beaufort at all is something of a mystery. The story is that the original owner of the mansion knew the Wertheimer family, or knew Sargent, or liked the portrait and bought the copy that eventually found its place at the entrance to the bar.

There are also rumors that it is the original while the one in the Tate is the copy.

At nearly five feet tall and more than three feet wide, the image is life size, and hung to suggest the subject's natural height, so trying to shake his hand or slap him on the back was a natural reaction. Old Asher's benevolent presence ensured that everyone entering the bar would be in a good mood.

While called a bar, there really was no bar. There was a semi-circular serving area with no stools. There always seemed to be the exact number of bar staff and waiters needed, presided over by Jason, the *chef de bar*, who had been there for as long as I can remember. (The Beaufort did not approve of females working in the bar. Women were welcome as guests, residents or customers off the street, but the bar staff was male.)

Though I probably stayed there only twice a year, I'd been doing that for more than twenty years and was always greeted as one of the Beaufort family. It was also true that at least once during my stay, I'd encounter someone I knew, invariably in the Asher Bar.

If there was no one there I knew, someone interesting usually presented himself.

ꙮ

The maritime conference was normally a two-day affair, but this year, because no one in the business had seen one another in over a year, it stretched to three-and-a-half days.

In ordinary years, it attracted about 175 people, but this year, more than 250 had signed up. It was still small enough to fit into one of the larger hotel ballrooms. This year, it would be at the Belgravia, conveniently a short walk from the Beaufort.

There would be a plenary session on Monday, with updates of the commercial outlook, changes in maritime law and practices, a summary of who had gone out of business, and developments in port facilities. During the evening, there would be dinner at the hotel.

The second day, two of the hotel's ballrooms would be set up for meetings with shippers, marine insurers, paint companies, instrument suppliers, and ship brokers. Typically, most of the appointments will have been made weeks in advance, but a few slots were kept open for spontaneous business.

On the third morning, there would be a brunch buffet with continuing discussions and a final wrap up.

I tell you this so that you will appreciate how retreating to the Asher Bar was both restful and necessary.

I arrived in New York mid-afternoon Sunday and checked into my room. Given enough notice, the hotel would automatically book guests into a room where they'd stayed previously.

After hanging my clothes and having a refreshing shower, I went down to the bar to see if any other delegates to the conference were staying there. A few did, and it was usually good to see them.

Smiling at Mr. Wertheimer on the way in, I found a chair, sat down and looked around. Few things had changed. The paneling, the gleaming brass and the carefully lit paintings were all the same. The curtains and carpet may have changed, but they were so unobtrusive, I couldn't be certain.

I had just ordered a Metroliner when a woman came in and began complaining to one of the waiters. Being a New Yorker, she wasn't subtle.

"That man out there burnt a hole in my scarf!" she said, holding up the smoldering silk.

I waited for her to tell everyone where it came from and how much it cost.

She did.

"And how did this happen?" asked Jason, who had materialized to ameliorate the situation.

"Obviously, he bumped into me with his cigar!" she said, impatiently, showing the scarf again.

He went into the corridor, followed by the woman, to see if anyone was around. It was a non-smoking hotel, so it seemed unlikely that a cigar-smoker would get very far without being stopped.

Jason said a few quiet words to the woman, and judging by his gestures, he was advising her to report the incident at the front desk.

Jason delivered my drink himself, and apologized for the delay.

"I saw that you had a fire to put out," I said.

He smiled, but said nothing indiscreet.

"Everyone's pretty vigilant about smoking," he said, "but it was a serious burn, and still warm."

He put the drink down and left me in peace.

That evening, I went out for a meal at a small taverna on Lexington, and on my return to the hotel, I took my notebook down to the bar and reviewed the meetings I would have during the next few days and refined some questions I wanted answers to.

Over the next few hours, I had only two drinks, and enjoyed working in the ambience of the bar. It was quiet at around eleven when I ordered my second drink. I noticed that my waiter from the afternoon was still on duty.

I commented on his long shift.

"I have a break for a meal when guests leave the bar for dinner," he said. "Then it picks up again."

"No more burnt clothing?" I ventured.

"No, sir," he said, then added, "but it's not the first curious incident we've had recently."

"Oh?"

"You know the Beaufort, sir, so you won't put stock in such things, but last week, someone complained of the smell of cigar smoke near the elevators and the bar entrance."

I laughed.

"Ha! Old Asher's cigar, I expect. It's the power of suggestion," I said, still chuckling.

"Indeed, sir. That's what we all thought until today, sir."

"No. The power of suggestion didn't burn that scarf."

☙

I had an early start, so I said good night to the bar staff and went to my room. The noises of cities are surprisingly distinct. Paris, even when it is very busy, has a completely different sound to the muffled, but penetrating sounds of London. New Orleans noise always has music in it somewhere, and in Boston, the noise of the traffic has a layer of whispering beneath it, expressing horror at the lack of decorum. New York noise is just noise: raw, jagged and unashamed, like art deco designs fragmented into abstraction.

The consequence was that while I slept in Paris and London with my windows open, in New York, they were shut – often because they wouldn't open or weren't designed to be.

Fortified by a good breakfast, I went to the Belgravia, collected my badge and conference papers, had another cup of coffee and looked around to see who was there.

It was a great feeling to shake hands with old colleagues and participate in face-to-face conversations, rather than stare at screens of faces that resembled talking stamp albums.

It was a long day of presentations and breakout sessions, punctuated with several breaks for coffee, lunch and finally a reception before dinner. This is only relevant to illustrate that when I returned to the Beaufort, I was tired and was ready for a quiet whisky.

No one was in the corridor when I stepped out of the elevator, and as I entered the bar, I yielded to the youthful temptation to smile at the portrait and say, "Good evening, Asher," as I went in.

There were a dozen people dotted about, singly, in couples and in groups. I stopped at the bar, said good evening to the bartender, and ordered my whisky.

The chair I had occupied the day before was empty and I resumed my place, picking a newspaper off the table before sitting down.

It was a different waiter to the one the night before who brought my drink. I started to read the newspaper, but was tired, and instead focused on the painting on the wall just across from me. It was a copy of Colin Campbell Cooper's painting of the public library. I only know it was a Cooper because I had read the label on an earlier visit, but it looked perfectly at home here.

It didn't take me long to finish my drink, and with all seeming to be in order in the Asher Bar, I went to my room.

ꕤ

After another early start and a breakfast to sustain me until the finger-food lunch, I went to drop my key at the desk and found a woman with her daughter, a girl of about ten, bending the ear of the receptionist.

"I don't expect to find stray dogs wandering the halls when I come out of my room in the morning," she was saying. "I didn't think pets were allowed in this hotel."

"He was nice," the girl said. "He just wanted to play."

"I'll send someone to have a look. You're on the second floor, aren't you, Mrs. Winters?"

"Go wash your hands, Cynthia," the woman commanded "You've had that unknown animal slobbering all over you."

I nodded at the clerk and put my key on the counter. He raised his head in acknowledgement and quickly returned to Mrs. Winters.

Before I was out of earshot, I heard the girl say, "It wasn't an unknown animal. His name is Noble. It was on his collar."

"I don't care if his name was Fiorello LaGuardia," her mother snapped. "Go wash your hands."

ℌ

On Wednesday, I entered the Belgravia for the last session. Tuesday's session had been good, but long, and when I returned to the Beaufort, I retreated to my room.

This morning, the lobby was congested with journalists and flunkies surrounding a man making polite, informative comments about the hotel and tourism in New York.

He was in his late forties, but had a gravitas not usually acquired for another fifteen or twenty years. Though he looked familiar, I didn't recognize him as being part of our conference, but I don't know everyone.

It wasn't until the mid-morning coffee break that an old contact, Lucius Fretwell, asked, "Did you see Martin Draycott downstairs this morning?"

"Of Draycott Destinations?"

"The same. He bought this hotel two years ago and modernized it," Fretwell said, treating 'modernized' as a four-letter word. "It used to be rather nice."

I considered this. Indeed, most of the detail had been removed, and vast expanses of wall were covered with inoffensive curtains. Light fittings were bright, but basic. I'd never been to the Belgravia before, but the contrast between the beaux arts exterior and the basic interior was striking.

"So that's who it was, clogging the lobby," I said. "I brokered the purchase of one of his cruise ships a few years back. The *Draycott Caribbean*. Used to be the *Mardi Gras Princess*, and before that the *Schloss Ettal*."

Fretwell burst out laughing.

"And before that, I sold it as the *Linderhof,*" he exclaimed. "It must have been about forty years old when Draycott bought it."

"From what I heard, he only invested enough to satisfy the safety specifications," I said. "Everything else was a coat of paint and some new linen."

"Call it 'minimalist' and it's fashionable."

"Did you deal with Draycott?" Fretwell asked.

"No. I worked with his development company."

"I guess the company's too big now for him to do it all," Fretwell observed. "Still, he retains a very hands-on approach to his acquisitions. He's a good businessman, and agreeable enough, if – *quirky*."

"Quirky?"

Fretwell considered his choice of word.

"Not long after the *Linderhof* sale, I contacted him about buying the *Agde Flamarens*," Fretwell related.

The collapse of Agde Cruises had made international headlines: ships out of food and fuel, and passengers stranded around the world. The French government was forced to step in to repatriate passengers and take possession of the ships.

The company had been doing well, and customer satisfaction was high, but its owner was caught with a cash-flow problem in 2009 and shifted his investment strategy to the Casino in Monte Carlo.

"The *Flamarens* was a good ship, and apart from the pilfering by the passengers and the crew who were afraid of not getting any money, it was in very good condition," Fretwell said. "Did you ever sell that one?"

"That was the old *Francisco Crispi*, wasn't it?"

"That's it," Fretwell nodded. "I sent the specifications to Draycott, but the gambling and subsequent suicide of the previous owner made him regard the ship as tainted in some way. He has an aversion to anything he believes is in any way *soiled*.

"He sent me a very nice personal note, thanking me for thinking of him, but I haven't done anything for him since."

"I guess you were tainted by association with the *Flamerens*?" I joked.

Fretwell looked serious.

"I told you, he's quirky."

☙

The remainder of the conference went well. I finished with lunch with a prospective new client and our meeting was interesting. He had seen a niche for smaller – even small – container ships that could access smaller, cheaper ports and was looking for ships that could be configured to serve that market.

It was an interesting concept that could revitalize some old ports and provide much-needed jobs just about everywhere. What he needed – in addition to the ships – was substantial backing to fund what was a pretty speculative proposition.

Our lunch meeting stretched until nearly four o'clock when my new client left to catch a flight. I had a sheaf of specifications and other material to review, and a long way to go before any ships were purchased.

When I returned to the Beaufort, I was pretty satisfied with the success of my visit. I had three pieces of business: one from an old customer, one from a newer one, and the potential of my newest one. One sale with any of them would pay for more than a year at the Beaufort.

Back in my room, I read the papers again sent some emails and made a few phone calls. By the time I'd finished, I was hungry and went down to the dining room, forgoing a preprandial drink.

The food at the Beaufort was reliable. It was not gourmet, not innovative, not pretentious: it was the sort of food that bridged eating at home and going to one of New York's fashionable restaurants. If no one was excited by it, nor was anyone disappointed. The service matched that of the rest of the hotel: properly done, but friendly.

I was eating a smoked haddock terrine and enjoying a glass of Chablis when I noticed, at the far end of the dining room, Martin Draycott. His presence told me that he was, most likely, the prospective buyer referred to by Francis when I checked in.

The thought nearly put me off my food until the main course arrived with the customary, "I hope it's the way you like it, sir," used for repeat guests.

Following the meal, I went into the bar (not failing to greet Asher on my way in) and ordered a drink. The bar was comfortably full, but there was time for a few words with the bar tender.

"Any more shaggy dog stories or signs of smoke?" I asked, lightly.

"Not today, sir," Jason, the *chef de bar,* answered, who had stepped through the door from the kitchen and heard my remark.

He dropped his voice.

"We have a special guest tonight," he said, nodding towards the corner.

Martin Draycott was seated there with a drink, reading a newspaper.

"Carrying out due diligence," I said. "I saw him in the dining room."

Jason said nothing, but gave a slight nod.

"If I may, sir?" Jason asked, conspiratorially.

"Of course," I replied.

"I believe you were at the front desk this morning and overheard the lady mistakenly complaining about a stray dog," he said.

"I was."

"Did you, by chance, hear the young lady's comment about the supposed dog?"

"She said it had a name."

"Indeed, she called it 'Noble,'" he said. He lowered his voice still further. "As a long-time guest at the Beaufort, you might be aware that the name of Mr. Wertheimer's black poodle in the portrait was called Noble."

I was not aware, but tried not to show it. This lent a new dimension to the smell of smoke and the burnt scarf.

"I'll bring your drink over," Jason said, returning to his normal voice, and I moved to one of the pair of armchairs not far from the bar.

I picked up a copy of the *New Yorker* and began to leaf through it, reading the cartoons. As I did, I saw that Martin Draycott had left his chair and looked like he was leaving the bar. He nodded and said goodnight to several people on his way, but then, struck by an idea, I stood up and took a step towards him.

He turned to me and smiled easily.

"Good evening," he said, convivially.

"Good evening, Mr. Draycott," I said. "I don't want to delay you," I said, producing a business card. "Not long ago, I sold your organization a cruise ship, and I might have an idea for you if you would be interested in getting into freight."

He took the card and I turned back to my chair.

"What ship?" he asked.

"The *Draycott Caribbean*."

"The old *Mardi Gras Princess.* Good ship," he said. "It's been very popular."

"I'm glad to hear it."

"Do you have time to outline the freight idea?" he asked.

"I do," I said, pleased that the bait had been taken.

"I'm leaving tomorrow around noon," he said. "If it's of interest, I'll follow up when I get back to Atlanta."

As we sat down, Jason delivered my drink and asked Draycott if he wanted another, but he declined.

"I wouldn't have thought of you for a freight proposition," I began, except I happened to see you at the Belgravia this morning."

"You were at the maritime conference."

"Yes. At the end of it, I had a meeting with a gentleman who's had an innovative idea that could benefit smaller ports," I said, feeling that this gave sufficiently little away.

"Is this what is called 'an investment opportunity'?" he asked, with a knowing smile.

"I know it's outside your usual territory, but your experience in shipping might make it interesting," I said. "As I said, you wouldn't have been on my radar for this had I not seen you at the Belgravia."

He considered this as I sipped my whisky. I also gazed around the bar in the hope of provoking a comment about the Beaufort.

One of the tricks in business – and in life – is to be able to leverage the one or two things you know, or can do, to maximum advantage.

While Draycott was thinking about freight shipping, I decided to interject a little distraction.

"I was surprised to see you here, sir," I began. "I assumed you'd be staying at the Belgravia."

"I am," he said. "It's essential to stay in hotels to ensure they're up to standards," he replied.

"I imagine so. Do you take cruises, too?"

He smiled.

"I do. I can't get on every ship every year. I have a team who does that, but I travel for one or two stops on half a dozen ships each year."

I remained impressed with his direct and engaging personality. There were hundreds of people who hated this man, but quite a few who admired what he did and were happy to work for him. Draycott Destinations had been listed in the top ten best companies to work for for a long time.

"So, visiting the Beaufort is to see how the competition is doing?"

"A bit of that. It's an interesting place and a brilliant location," he said. "The Belgravia's location is one of its greatest assets and it's always full."

It was a statement of fact, not a boast.

It was now or never.

"Well, if you ever wanted to offer something different, the Beaufort can certainly offer it."

I took a drink, then spoke again.

"There are a number of smaller freighters on the market that make my client's proposition look viable," I said. "I haven't had time to do a full analysis – I only met the man this afternoon – "

Draycott waved his hand.

"Yes, send me a proposal, it sounds like something we could be interested in. Now, what were you saying about the Beaufort being able to offer something different?"

The trap slammed shut.

As Fretwell had noted, the idea of a hotel with supernatural amenities, destroyed Draycott's interest in the Beaufort, and the acquisition was called off.

The hotel's owners were able to secure the necessary investment through the collaboration of several of its regular guests, who wanted nothing changed, and it continues as it has done for ninety years.

I did not pursue Martin Draycott, feeling that he would regard me as tainted by association, but he contacted me two weeks later asking where the proposal was, and we are now working together.

As for reports about dogs, the smell of cigar smoke and burnt scarves at the Beaufort, well, they disappeared with Draycott's interest.

Though, as I left the bar after my discussion with Draycott and passed into the corridor, I had the distinct sensation that a dog had licked my hand.

Making History

Making History

I was reminded the other day of an event from my youth when I was beginning to assist my father in his work. One of the great railway tunnelling projects in London –the Elizabeth Line (or Cross Rail or the Purple Line) – was delayed, yet again, because it had run into an ancient burial site. Whether it was a pauper's field, a plague pit or a Roman cemetery has not yet been determined.

Such occurrences are not uncommon in an ancient city, like London, where just about anything from badgers and newts to human remains and unexploded bombs can delay construction for years.

Today, every construction project has a team of archaeologists standing by, from the local authority, the construction company itself, or special interest groups. The success of the Richard III Society in locating that king's final resting place has elevated the influence of such groups for the foreseeable future.

Things were not always like that and, in the mid-sixties, people had a better sense of priorities and recognised that to deny the present and future for the past was not always practical – or even a good idea.

This leads me to my father. He had been with the Royal Corps of Engineers during World War II –"when engineers could get on with their jobs" – and, on his separation from the Army as a major, he began working with a small construction company.

It prospered, and by the time I was in my late teens, it had expanded and been bought by one of the country's larger firms. As a result, my father – who, when working with him, I refer to as "the major" – rose to a senior position. At the time I write about, he was in charge (on the ground, not in the office) of a project to bring greater energy capacity into the City of London. This involved digging a lot of holes, tunnels and trenches.

At the time, I was still living at home and working on one of my first engineering qualifications. Part of that training was practical, and I was working with my father. While an arrangement that would not have worked for everyone, working with the major was an amazing experience. At work, he was tough, but once off the clock, he'd review the day with me and help me over the difficulties I'd faced. Some were to do with engineering, but most were in dealing with people. His experience of command – albeit limited command – gave him a fearlessness in demanding high standards, discipline and everyone's focus on the job. This extended to me.

One day on the job, the major lit into me in a way that even some of the rough workers commiserated. “He’s a tough bastard, but he’s a fair bastard. I’ll work for him any day.” That caused my pride in him to exceed the fury of my misery.

One autumn night, the telephone rang at about two in the morning. I dragged myself into the upstairs hallway to answer it.

It was the Metropolitan Police asking for my father.

Reluctantly, I woke him. While not common, he did receive such calls. Usually it was about someone breaking into the company’s on-site tool storage locker, or once, someone, after a night at the pub, had stolen a Caterpillar D6 medium-sized bulldozer and was joy-riding around Reading.

“That says a lot about Reading if the only joy to be had is driving a D6,” my father had said to the police, before getting in his car and heading out.

This time, I watched him as he took the message. As he listened, his eyes opened wide and something of a smile formed, though his voice remained gravely serious.

When he hung up, after numerous yes sirs, he told me to get dressed – warmly. He also told me to get all the large plastic bags I could find and bring torches.

Once in the car and heading out from our home near Highgate, he told me that we were headed to Camberwell.

"The police in Camberwell had a complaint about some lads playing footie with human skulls in an area where we're dumping earth from the London site."

While inconvenient, this was worth getting up for.

"I'll have to work out exactly which location it came from and sort things out that end, but for now, we should collect what we can find, secure the site and come back in daylight to make sure we've got everything."

I was surprised that he didn't seem more annoyed, but I suppose he just took this as another part of his work.

The major knew London like the back of his hand, and while he could have navigated side roads and back streets, at this time of the morning it was a clear run down Archway, the Caledonian Road, Gray's Inn Road, cut over Holborn, then down Farringdon Street and over Blackfriars Bridge. Once over the river, I had less idea where I was, but I think we went through Elephant and Castle before eventually reaching Camberwell.

My father knew exactly where the dumping site was, itself the location for another new block of concrete flats, and pulled up to the open gates. A lone constable stood by the entrance looking bored and cold.

Once he identified himself, we pulled the car into the yard and broke out the torches and plastic bags.

"I've got chains and a new lock," my father said to the constable. "If you want to get back to the station, we'll close up."

The policeman looked dubious. My father gave him a business card.

"Thank you for your help, and thank the boys at the station," he said, in his major's voice.

Used to following anything that sounded remotely like an order, the constable trousered the card, and touched his helmet.

"Thank you, sir. Goodnight."

"Right. Let's get to work," my father said.

We found a few skulls and bagged them, but finding anything else in the rubble that included wood and metal was impossible in the dark, so we put the bags in the boot, secured the gate and headed home, arriving in time to have a few hours' sleep.

I knew I'd be the one to be sent to do the clean up, and I'd have to get there early, otherwise the men would be locked out of the site. I'd have to prevent any more dumping, but my father was hoping to identify the source of the bones and stop further deliveries.

This worked, and I spent the morning turning over a lorry-load of earth and picking bones and fragments from it. There seemed to have been only one load with bones and using an iron rake that I had thought to put in the car, I was able to make a fairly thorough search.

The men assigned to the site had nothing to do and assisted in the search, for which I was grateful. It was novel, and they kept up a steady stream of jokes and puns as we filled the bags.

I drove back into the City and parked in an expensive garage. Rather than wander the streets with bags of bones, I left them in the car.

During the morning, the police had notified the City authorities and some official was at the site when I arrived. My father had one of those site offices that looked like it was made from an articulated lorry (this was before the day of shipping containers) and waved me in when I appeared in the doorway.

"This is Mr Burtwhistle," he said. "He's just been explaining that we can't simply re-bury the bones here."

Burtwhistle was one of those officials who would contradict you if you said, "Good morning."

"That's not strictly true. You can bury them when you've obtained a burial permit."

My father nodded patiently, and I could see how I'd be spending the afternoon.

"Where are the bones now," Burtwhistle asked.

"In the boot of the car in Smithfield Car Park," I said.

Burtwhistle shook his head.

"That won't do. Unless you're a licensed hearse or hospital or police vehicle you can't be driving human remains around the country," he said.

"What do you suggest?" the major asked, with more patience than I expected.

"The bones should be in a proper morgue or undertakers," he said. "That could be a police morgue or a hospital morgue."

My father thought.

"I know a doctor at St Bart's," he said. "Would it be acceptable for him to store them until we get the paperwork?"

Burtwhistle didn't exactly smile, but he looked well-satisfied.

"That would be satisfactory," he said.

"And when I get the permit, we can re-inter the bones here, where they came from," the major said.

Burtwhistle nodded.

"It's not required, but if you know a vicar, saying a prayer over them might appease City officials and smooth public relations."

My father nodded.

"If you register the death at the Islington and London City Register Office, they will issue a burial permit," Burtwhistle said.

"Have you had lunch?"

I shook my head.

We went to a pub not far from Smithfield which had excellent steak sandwiches. It was a treat, but my father felt we deserved it for our interrupted night and curious day.

"What we dug into was a plague pit dating from 1665," he told me, after taking a deep drink of his bitter. "Apparently, it was ground that belonged to a defunct livery company that, like the Worshipful Company of Wood-mongers, had been overcharging for fuel and lost its charter in 1667. This one had been for an even more obscure trade like the hoof-trimmers, or bondlegroomers and had been stripped of its charter in about 1660. The land was in litigation, according to Burtwhistle, and simply seized for plague burials.

"The trouble was, that it wasn't tended and in a few generations was just regarded as vacant land and built on, several times. It was damaged during the war and became just another bombsite for redevelopment."

Getting to Islington Town Hall from Smithfield was possible only by bus or taxi. You can guess which option I was given.

After queuing for about forty minutes for the registrar, I went into the office. It looked like something from *Bleak House*.

"I would like a burial permit," I said.

The registrar motioned to a chair without looking up, and I sat down.

"We begin by registering the death," he said, opening his book of certificates.

"Name of deceased?"

"I have no idea."

Finally, he looked up.

"Don't waste my time young man," he said, sharply.

"Name of deceased," he repeated, looking down again.

"Unknown."

He sighed.

"Date of birth?"

"Unknown."

"Age at time of death?"

"Unknown."

"Sex?"

"I'm sorry?"

"Male or female."

"Yes."

"Which?"

"Probably both."

"I've warned you once," the registrar said, but he still would not let me explain.

"Do you know anything?" he asked, in desperation.

"I have a bag of bones that I need a permit to re-bury," I finally managed to say.

"There's a long story here, isn't there?" he said, taking off his glasses and pinching his nose. "I fill in forms. Usually, there's not more than a dozen blanks to fill in, and it's not badly paid. I don't like long stories.

"All right. What *do* you know?"

"Cause of death," I ventured.

"All right," he replied, tentatively. "What was the cause of death?"

"Probably bubonic plague."

I could tell he was trying hard not to throw me out.

"Date of death?"

"Probably 1665."

He looked up again. His face was flushed.

"You know you are required to report a death within five days. Eight in Scotland, but this is tardy even for the Scots.

"Where are the bones now?" he asked.

"On their way to St Bart's morgue," I answered, confidently, hoping it was true.

He nodded.

"I'll have to look into this," he said. "Come back next week."

I gave him my name and address, and my father's name and company details.

When I got back to the site, it was growing dark and the men were stowing their tools.

I told my father of my lack of success.

"I had slightly better luck," he said. "I collected the bones from the car and took them to George Bell at St Bart's. He agreed to put them in the morgue."

ஐ

There were no more calls from the police and work proceeded until the next week when I went back to Islington.

"Things are looking up," the registrar said, with an actual smile. "Your query has now been passed up three levels."

"That's great news!" I exclaimed, trying to echo his delight. "When do you expect an answer?"

His face lost its smile.

"I'm not really sure," he said. "I've never received anything from that high up before, but I've only been here fourteen years."

I revisited Islington each week for the next three weeks, then extended the interval to three weeks, then four.

Then, one day shortly before Easter, my father had a phone call to say that the permit had been approved. I was despatched *poste haste* to collect it. My father would go to St Bart's and retrieve the bones and we could have them back in the ground before nightfall.

In Islington, the registrar looked very pleased, and handed over the permit with commensurate gravitas.

"This will need to be signed and sealed by the person officiating, and then returned, by him or you," he said.

I thanked him formally, put the permit in my jacket pocket, and treated myself to a taxi back to the site.

When I arrived, my father wasn't as pleased as I was.

"I went round to St Bart's to collect the bones and George said that he thought we'd forgotten about them and sent them for disposal with other human remains."

He shrugged and turned back to the plans he'd been studying.

"I've got to return this permit with the endorsement of a priest, undertaker, or doctor," I said.

The major waved his hand, "Just take it back before the end of the week. It will be good to be done with this nonsense."

I accepted defeat. It had been an interesting experience in how government officials operate, but it had also been a colossal waste of time.

On Friday afternoon, I took the bus back to Islington and sat outside the registrar's office.

When I was called in, it was a different registrar to the one I'd been dealing with. He had gone on leave. While missing the familiarity, I thought it might be easier to deal with someone who hadn't been put out by the process.

"I have a burial permit that is now superfluous to requirement that I wish to return."

I had practised that line on the bus, and was pleased with the syntax.

The new man took it from me and read it.

"Rose from the dead did they?" he asked. "Took rather a long time to do it."

I wasn't pleased with this attitude, but was prepared to endure it just to have done with the episode.

The registrar stood up and held the permit out to me.

"This is a permit to bury human remains, and human remains you must bury! And let me know when you have, with the form duly endorsed."

At that moment, I could think of only one candidate whose remains I would like to see buried in a plague pit.

The major would not be pleased.

If this is what a life in engineering involved, I thought I might do something else, like teach physics.

My father was not as bothered as I expected when I told him of the registrar's instructions and gave him the unsigned application.

"I'll see what I can do," he said, calmly, and went back to work.

Work progressed normally the next week, and the team was getting ready to cover the final part of excavation, more than a hundred feet from where the bones had originally been extracted. Electricity, gas, water and telephone lines had all been re-routed, tested and reinstated.

A delay could be costly, but my father was cheerful as things were otherwise on schedule and on budget (a remarkable thing in 1960s Britain).

On the morning that the final bit of trench would be closed, the major said, “Let’s see about those bones.”

Together we walked over to St Bart’s and called at a back door, used for staff. Inside, the porter rang for Dr Bell who arrived a few minutes later with two black plastic bags and handed them to me. He handed an envelope to my father.

My father thanked him, said he owed him a drink or three, and we headed back to the site.

We left the bones in the bag, and I went down the ladder into the hole. My father passed them down, and I carefully laid them next to the yellow gas pipe. Looking at the walls of the trench, even there, I could see the odd bone, broken by the digger, and briefly wondered about the lives and terrible death those people might have had.

My family wasn’t particularly religious, but my father and I both paused to say a prayer. The Irishman who operated the digger knew what was going on and climbed off the machine, took off his hat and blessed himself before returning to the cab and starting the engine.

After a moment, the major barked, "Close it up!"

We watched the trench be filled in to ground level, and the surface smoothed before walking back to the office cabin.

"One more trip to Islington," he said, handing me the envelope. "We could post it, but I'm not leaving anything to chance on this one."

I opened it to ensure that this would not be a wasted trip. Dr Bell had endorsed it with his signatures and all his qualifications: MB, ChB, FRCS, and embossed with the hospital's seal.

"There's no arguing with this," I said, putting it in my pocket. "But I thought the bones were gone?"

"Engineers learn that there's more than one way to do things," my father said. "After a good lunch with George last week, he went round to Smithfield market and collected a few bags of sheep and cow bones and certified them as human."

"Couldn't he get in trouble for that?" I asked, my naiveté shocked.

"Yes, but who's going to tell?" my father said, with a twinkle. "When you deliver that, you'll be complicit in the fraud."

"But – "

"Think of it as a small contribution to history, and imagine what the archaeologists will think in four hundred years."

City of Spirits

City of Spirits

Ciutat dels Esperits

Homentage a Carlos Ruiz Zafon

Foreigners were fairly uncommon when I was growing up in a small Pennsylvania city. People had pretty standard first and last names, usually German, Irish or British. So, when a girl called Montserrat Bruguera turned up among the Patsy Stottlemyer, Beth Hostetter, Jackie Beamesderfer, Rosie Ritter, Mary Casey, Mary Frances O'Brien and Mary Beth Reillys of the school, it was like being visited by someone from another world.

Our first assumptions were that she was from some South American country, or more exotically, Spain. Montserrat made it very clear that her family was Catalan. Her family included a sister, Nuria ("Noor-ya"), her mother, Francesca, and her father, Albert.

My father knew Mr. Bruguera from business. My father was a lawyer and did property work for the company Mr. Bruguera worked for. Both Mr. and Mrs. Bruguera used to attend the few parties that my parents gave, one around Christmas, and one in the summer. These were adult parties and the girls never came, though my mother used to see Mrs. Bruguera fairly often around town and they were members of the same bridge and book clubs. On occasion, it would be hosted at the Bruguera's' and my mother would see the girls.

Apart from their distinctly European looks, both Montserrat and Nuria were nice enough, but tended to keep to themselves. Montserrat was dark with striking eyes and good features, while Nuria was blonde, but, I thought, not particularly interesting looking.

The only curious thing was that in all the years we were at school together and our parents were friends, my mother never suggested that I take out Montserrat.

My mother was always promoting one or another of her friends' daughters: pretty, talented, interesting, bubbly (one of her favorite words), or, a good tennis player, likes to dance, paints well, or any other attractive attribute that she could think of.

Given the schools we went to and the size of the city, it was inevitable that I'd go out with girls whose parents my parents knew. Often, my parents and mine had been to high school with each other, and perhaps gone to dances, movies and things together. If they did, they had the good sense not to tell me. It's not the sort of thing that children want to know.

This would not have been true, of course, with the Brugueras as they arrived when Monserrat was in fifth grade.

She and I were friendly enough, but I only saw her in a group, at parties and school events. At parties, we'd occasionally dance with each other but never spent any time together.

That was until our senior year.

ಡ

We had chance meetings twice during that year and took the opportunity to talk. The first time was in the spring when I was cutting through the park and got caught in a thunderstorm. With no shelter around, I went into the small Victorian bandstand and found Montserrat sheltering there, too. With the benches around the edge of the stand soaking wet, we sat on the low raised stage and waited for the storm to pass.

I thought that the rain would let up enough to continue home in about five minutes, but the torrential rain continued, so we talked. We didn't talk about anything too significant. Mostly school, friends in common, music, disagreements with our parents, college plans – normal stuff.

She sounded vague about her college plans. I didn't press too hard, but asked for some details.

"I can trust you, can't I?" she asked.

"I think so."

"I've hardly told anyone and I've asked them not to say anything," she explained. "My parents are moving back to Spain. I'll be going to university there. I've been accepted at the University of Salamanca."

From outback Pennsylvania, this sounded unbelievably exotic. Salamanca. It sounded magical, mostly because I had no idea where it was. I thought it was in Spain, but it could have been the next town to Casablanca for all I knew.

"What will you study?"

"English and Spanish literature," she said. "If I continue with the English, I can probably get a university teaching position."

She told me about the university. It was founded in 1134. I couldn't imagine that far back.

"Is it far from Barcelona?" I asked, desperate to keep the conversation going.

"Ten hours if you stop for lunch," she said. "Just head for Portugal and you'll get there," she joked.

"Are you looking forward to it?"

She hesitated for the first time.

"It's very different there," she said, eventually.

The storm had passed, and Montserrat and I said goodbye and went home.

I continued to see her at school and we'd say "Hi" as we passed in the corridors, but there was nothing more.

About a week before graduation, we had our second encounter. It was almost exactly like the first in that one Saturday afternoon, we met crossing the same park. I was on my way to go shopping, and Montserrat was on her way home. We were approaching the bandstand as our paths converged and we exchanged a few words of greeting, but before passing the bandstand and returning to our separate paths, Monserrat asked:

"Do you have a minute?"

I nodded, and she walked up the steps and sat on the platform where we had been before.

"I wanted to say that I'm telling people now about going to Spain," she said.

"I heard you were going to Barnard."

"That was just a story until my parents' plans were settled and everything was in place for Salamanca," she said. "Thank you for keeping the secret. I really appreciate it."

I shrugged.

"No," she protested. "It's important to be able to trust people. I regretted taking the chance telling you before I got home, but you kept your word."

"Are you looking forward to it now?"

She didn't reply immediately.

"It will be a different life."

"It must be more interesting than living here," I said. "Whoever came up with the term Nowheresville must have been from here."

Montserrat laughed, and I realized how little I'd seen her laugh. It was a deep, dark, rich laugh, wholly unlike that of the silly girls at school. It struck me as being a laugh born of experience, or a different *knowing* than that found among the natives of Bucks County.

That discovery suddenly opened my eyes to what it really meant to be foreign; to have completely different reference points to your life; different allegiances; different ways of looking at the things my classmates and I looked at every day.

"Are you from Barcelona itself?" I asked, having looked up "Catalan."

"Not far from it," she replied. "It's where my father's job will be. I expect they'll live in the city, which means I will, too."

I had no picture in my mind of Barcelona. I knew nothing about it. It was as amorphous as Salamanca, and sounded just as exotic.

"I'll be glad to leave here," I said. "I'm going to New England for college."

That was foreign to me.

"Yes," Montserrat said. "I heard you were going to Bates. That's supposed to be good."

"We'll see."

She reached for her shopping bag.

"Let me know how you get on," I said. "I'd love to hear about a European university."

"Okay," she replied. "Give my best to your parents."

And we went home. I relayed Montserrat's greeting over dinner. Mother looked suspicious, but my father noted that it was a very European thing to extend greetings to families.

My final encounter was very brief. It was at the school prom. Monserrat had invited a boy from another school. Not unheard of, but not that common. He had gone to get refreshments and my date had gone to help one of her girlfriends through some crisis.

Montserrat approached me. She looked very striking, but not in an American high school way.

"We both seem to have been abandoned," she said to me.

"Would you like to dance?" I asked.

"Your date won't kill you?"

"She might whether we dance or not."

Montserrat laughed and we enjoyed a brief dance and were able to exchange a few words before I returned her to her table.

As she sat down, she continued to hold my hand and said, "I meant what I said in the park. It's important to be able to trust people."

And that was the last I saw of her for twenty-five years.

ཀ

We wrote a few short letters to each other while at college before settling into the annual exchange of

Christmas cards. Monserrat always added a few lines to say how she was doing.

Unexpectedly, one summer when I was in my mid-twenties, I had a postcard from her in Greece telling me that she'd been married. Her husband, Ricard, from a Catalan family, was a businessman in Barcelona. They'd met when she had a summer job at a restaurant while she was a student at Salamanca.

My life moved on and as my career developed, I did more and more travelling, mostly to Europe. My trips were usually short with little time for socializing, so although I had been to Spain, I didn't have time for side trips to Barcelona or visits with old friends. International business travel bears very little resemblance to that in old Jack Lemon films or episodes of *The Saint*.

Montserrat and I continued to exchange Christmas cards and mentioned the possibility of meeting up one day. Her cards always had some news, sometimes of mutual friends. She would also include the names of films and books that had interested her.

Finally, one year, when I was in my late thirties, I found Barcelona on my work schedule several times. I contacted Montserrat and offered to meet them for dinner, lunch, or just coffee or drinks.

On each occasion, she was away on holiday or travelling with her husband. On one occasion, we managed a phone call. Apart from a stronger accent, she sounded much the same. She encouraged me to keep trying as she thought it would be fun and even hinted that her husband and I might be able to do some business together.

She repeated as much in her Christmas card that year. I mentioned it to my mother, who was surprised we were still in touch. I had kept in contact with a lot of school friends, and said so, but she was skeptical and said nothing.

Later that year, Montserrat sent me a postcard saying that she would be in London for two weeks, and gave the dates.

"On the off-chance that your travels might take you there."

In fact, they did.

Both of us retained enough of our younger looks that we had no trouble recognizing each other when we met in a large hotel bar. Montserrat looked elegant; her clothes were well cut and her European style of makeup made her look very intriguing.

Yet, her smile was the same. She kissed my cheeks – which few Americans are comfortable with – and for the next hour talked brightly but told me virtually nothing.

Her husband was there on business, and she was doing some buying for an unspecified enterprise where she worked, but as an employee, manager or owner, she didn't say. I was very curious, but didn't know her well enough to pry.

She was also teaching at both ends of the spectrum. She had a good job at the university where she taught English literature, but she also spent time teaching anyone who needed it to read and write. This took her to some of Barcelona's poorest neighborhoods, and I admired her bravery and commitment. When I commented on the danger, she merely shrugged.

I focused my conversation on Barcelona: what I had seen, how I loved the atmosphere and food; and had come to know the city as well as any other city I visited, at home or abroad.

While Montserrat made sounds of agreement with my enthusiasm for Barcelona, she offered little in the way of real comment. It wasn't until later that I realized how little she had offered about her adopted city.

She spoke about her husband but was vague about his business. Travel and food appeared to be the topics that interested her most.

Inevitably, we went through the list of old classmates. She was in touch with only a few of us and displayed little interest in the ones she had not kept in touch with.

Curiously, none of this made our conversation awkward or formal. She spoke easily as she had in the bandstand: with sincerity and a modicum of affection.

We parted with her encouraging me to contact her the next time I was in Barcelona.

ꕥ

It was mid-summer when I received an envelope with a Spanish stamp on it. I recognized Montserrat's handwriting. It was not unusual to hear from her at this time of year, but it had always been a postcard with some wonderful Mediterranean view. This time, it was a more formal envelope of good quality paper. Though the change of format might have alerted me, it did not, so when I read the first few lines, I was taken off guard.

Montserrat's husband had been killed in a car accident in Italy. I was able to check the newspapers online and found that it had been a spectacular accident with her husband's car sailing off the road and crashing down a rocky cliff into the sea. At least one passenger was also killed; the article was vague and my Italian not up to much more than menus.

In her note, Montserrat said she had dealt with everything, and gone back to work part-time and continued to live at the same address.

She made it clear that she wanted to move forward and didn't want sympathy and concluded that, should I come to Barcelona, I not fail to get in touch.

Even with my cursory research into her husband's death, Montserrat's letter raised a lot of questions. I had no idea what work he did, and I had tried to find out.

The articles said, "businessman" (the more sensational said, "international businessman"). The way she simply stated her intention to move forward suggested either a total denial of her loss and the upset of her life, or an extraordinary insensibility to what had happened to her. Both were common enough, but in either case, I worried about her.

I satisfied myself in the knowledge that there was a trip to Spain penciled in for mid-September. I now resolved to ensure that it happened.

☙

My familiarity with Barcelona had grown over several trips from my familiarity with the Ramblas. It had been the trunk and my explorations of the branches had taken me into much of the central city.

I had stayed at various hotels, ancient and modern, along its length, later extending down the upper parts of La Avenida Diagonal. I had been going long enough to remember the Gothic Quarter before it was sanitized and made to look like a hundred other pedestrian shopping precincts before the 1992 Olympics. The cramped tapas bars and shops of the crowded, car-choked alleys were gone, replaced by Gucci, Prada, Hermès, and other irrelevancies.

Over subsequent visits, I had extended explorations to Montjuïc, Tibidabo, Parc del Laberint, Badalona, and later, up to Figueres to see the Dali Museum.

On this occasion, I was able to add an extra two days to ensure that I was able to see Montserrat. Vanity enabled me to think that seeing someone from her school days might help her through her grief, remind her of happier times, or at least be a diversion.

In the event, my business spilled over into an additional day and I was forced to call her and cancel lunch, but arranged to meet her for drinks at my hotel which had a congenial bar. I booked a table for nine-thirty (early for Barcelona) at the Restaurant 7 Portes. It was a tourist magnet, but a place that locals liked visit occasionally, too.

I expected to have had time to do some shopping and perhaps visit a museum or church that day, but by the time my meetings concluded, I had to rush back to the hotel, have a quick shower and change to be ready to meet Montserrat at seven.

She was in the bar drinking a cocktail when I eventually got downstairs. She was in black, not uncommon in Spain, and looked like a no-nonsense businesswoman, or it could have been mourning.

Her features softened when she saw me, and she stood as I approached.

I apologized for being late.

"I'm flattered you took the time to see me," she said, after kissing my cheeks.

A waiter came almost as soon as we sat down. Montserrat ordered another cocktail and I asked for a white Rioja.

"We've missed each other too much," I said, before realizing how this could be misinterpreted. "I've been here, you've been elsewhere," I added, awkwardly attempting to clarify.

"Well, I am here now, and expect to remain here," she said.

"I was so sorry to hear about Ricard," I said.

"Your letter was lovely."

The uneasy silence was relieved by the arrival of our drinks.

"Salut," she said, raising her glass.

"Cheers."

"How long are you here for?" Montserrat asked.

"My flight is tomorrow evening, around eight-thirty."

She nodded.

"Good. You can come to my house for lunch," she said, brightly.

We talked about a few old mutual friends, our parents – all four still alive – and my work. I then ventured to ask if she was working.

"Such as it is," she replied. "I work mostly at the library now. It's hardly demanding, but I enjoy it."

I waited for her to tell me more, but she didn't continue. I hoped the whole evening wasn't going to be punctuated with these silences, but looking at Montserrat, she appeared perfectly relaxed, even contented. She didn't look like she'd drifted into a dreamworld, nor did she look completely present.

"This is the first chance in weeks that I've had just to sit quietly, enjoy a drink and the company of an old friend," she said, at length.

Now, it was my turn to say nothing for a while. I don't expect it looked like I enjoyed the experience as much as she did.

The conversation returned and we ranged through the subjects we had discussed before, and then she returned to talking about Ricard.

"He was special. I was lucky we found each other," she mused.

"What did he do?" I asked, preferring to deal with facts rather than emotions. "Was he in Italy on business?"

Montserrat seemed to come out of a reverie and stared at me as if trying to remember the question.

"Italy?"

"Was Ricard in Italy on business?" I repeated.

Montserrat picked up her cocktail and looked at it before drinking some more.

"I suppose he must have been," she said, in a perfectly normal manner and put her glass down.

I tried not to look surprised or puzzled.

"Was he often away?"

"He was away more than he was here," she said, looking at me squarely. "That's what makes it so hard to believe that he's dead."

"Did he have many friends here?" I asked. "He was from Barcelona, wasn't he?"

"Friends?" she considered the word. "Not in the sense that you and I are friends, but he had many, very many, acquaintances."

She finished her cocktail.

"Would you like another, or would you like to go somewhere else?" I asked.

"Let's walk."

The evening was mild. The clocks had not yet gone back so it would be light for another hour. Watching the darkness creep in, and seeing the lights come on and redefine the city was something that I still found exciting. It was a daily unlocking of a different world, filled with unknown events and potential.

Bright windows gleamed with colorful dresses, sweaters, shirts and silk ties and scarves, leather goods, shoes, jewelry, bottles of wine and endless food: fruit, vegetables, fat legs of cured ham, trays of ice with fish and shellfish, thick pieces of beef, and *pastisseria*.

We walked by most, but occasionally Montserrat or I would stop for a closer look. I tried to read her thoughts based on which shops she stopped in front of, but it appeared to be random. She looked at some second-hand books on a cart in an alley, and read the menu at several restaurants (one Chinese, one Japanese, and several serving cured meats).

We came into a more crowded pedestrian area with upmarket shops, but she ignored the brands and looked into the window of a stationers.

"I like good paper and ink," she said.

"Do you like good pens?"

"I have one or two, but I tend to write with the cheap fountain pens one finds in the supermarkets," she said. "Write with them long enough and they either develop a good nib, or they wear down and cross."

"No Montblanc Meisterstück?" I teased.

She turned to me and smiled.

"Ricard had one," she said. "He loved it. It was a present from his father when he turned eighteen. He used it all through university."

She continued to smile at the memory.

"I suppose it went off the cliff with him. Pity."

Her almost satisfied expression disturbed me.

She then turned from the window and began walking on, taking my hand, which unnerved me even more.

We wandered in silence for a while. We had gone down the Ramblas and moved into Raval and moved in a circuitous route into the area once referred to by sailors as the "Chinese Quarter," or "The Gut." I still would not choose to walk here in the dark, but the shops and bars were busy and it had undergone some sanitizing since my first visit. Montserrat appeared to know it well and gave no hint of uneasiness.

She chose a tapas bar apparently at random. It appeared to have missed the sanitizing process completely as it was like the ones I remembered: small, crowded, smoke-filled, noisy and alive.

It had ancient stone walls and floors along with a high beamed ceiling from which, over the bar, hung dozens of legs of Serrano ham. While I was looking up, Montserrat had pushed up to the bar and ordered two glasses of wine and a small plate of ham.

We found the edge of a shelf to put our drinks on and I tasted a piece of the deep pink meat.

"Cheers," said Montserrat, clinking her glass to mine.

She was clearly at home in this place and looked around at the crowd. Then, she lifted her glass a little to indicate the ceiling.

"Some of those hams look like they have been there since before the Civil War," she said. "When I was here last, they unhooked one and put it on the bar. A cloud went up and *el cap* began scraping off years of dust and fat. It took a good ten minutes of scraping before the color of the ham began to show through, and another five minutes before it was ready to carve."

We ate, savoring the flavor and the atmosphere. Tapas are perfect for whetting the appetite, and when we set out for the restaurant, I knew I was ready to eat.

"Do you want to get a taxi?" I asked, as we emerged onto the Ramblas.

"It won't take long," Montserrat said. "In this city, one gets used to walking. The traffic is terrible and taxis are expensive."

I was happy to walk. We crossed into the Gothic Quarter. I knew this area well, but Montserrat surprised me.

"I'll show you where I work," she said, and turned into a passage that I didn't recognize. We walked for a bit and then turned into a smaller alley.

Montserrat pointed to a heavy carved oak door set into an ancient stone archway.

"That's the library," she said, proudly. "It's a pity it's not open. It's ancient and enormous. Some of the walls are Roman."

"Have you worked there long?"

"On and off, almost since I came to Barcelona," she said.

She looked up the high walls of the building admiringly.

"There are so many books in there, it's a pity more people don't use it."

I was about to ask her when it was open, so I could visit it in the morning if I had time, but she had turned and was heading out of the alley.

Almost as soon as we passed the library door, I saw an old bookdealer with large, ancient books with leather and worn cotton bindings next to his cart. I started to slow down, but Montserrat continued moving briskly towards the restaurant.

I knew the next street we turned into, or I thought I did. Where I thought I remembered an incongruous modern building, there were only old buildings in various states of disrepair. I broke loose to inspect an old doorway that was richly carved.

I caught up with Montserrat, and we proceeded through more narrow lanes until we turned onto a main street that led to Passeig d'Isabel II. We arrived at the restaurant at almost exactly nine-thirty.

"It's always good to come here," Montserrat said, when we were seated. "When you live here, you tend not to go to the best-known places even though they are very good."

I laughed, unsure if this were genuine or a slight on my pedestrian choice.

"Next time, I'll take you to Los Caracoles."

Montserrat laughed, but didn't look up from her menu.

"I'm going to start with the cannelloni and then have the baked goat," she said, and set her menu down.

I told her I'd be having the cod fritters and venison.

"Any preference for wine?" I asked.

"I'm a sucker for Marques de Riscal," I said.

"You are allowed to choose that," Montserrat replied. "You knew enough to order a white Rioja, so I know you know a little."

"I like the good Navarras, too," I said, laughing.

She nodded approval.

"It's nice to see foreigners who don't just order *tinto* or sangria."

I don't know what we talked about, but between the food and the conversation, the evening passed very quickly and, as I swirled my Carlos I, realized it was after midnight.

The service had been perfectly paced so that our meal stretched easily into the more traditional Spanish dinner time.

As we prepared to leave, Montserrat asked about the next day – or rather, later that day.

"If I come to your hotel around noon, would that be all right?" she asked. "You can leave your suitcase at the desk and collect it on your way to the airport."

"Wouldn't it be easier if I just came to your house?" I offered.

"I'll need to do some shopping and will be out. You'd never find it, anyway."

I didn't protest.

In the exchanges that Montserrat had with the waiter about coffee and drinks, I hadn't realized that she had also ordered a taxi, so when the waiter appeared to tell us it was time to go, I thought it a bit odd until I saw the taxi waiting.

"My house is beyond your hotel, up Passeig de Gràcia and over behind some large houses," she said in the taxi. "I'll make us a nice lunch."

"I'll take you out somewhere," I offered, aware that she was still holding my hand.

"No. My turn."

We gave each other the lightest of social kisses when I got out of the taxi.

Fortunately, the effects of the amount of alcohol I'd consumed were mitigated by the excellent meal. The idea of eating again in less than twelve hours was not yet appealing, besides, I had plenty of other things to think about.

Montserrat's reaction to her husband's death was surprising. They had been married for more than ten years, but she showed more sadness for the loss of a fountain pen that wasn't even hers.

Then, there was her general manner. She wasn't being overtly seductive, but after the initial stiltedness of our conversation, Montserrat warmed up and relaxed, and her whole demeanor suggested that we had been better friends than we ever were.

I thought more about this as I prepared for bed, and lay awake struggling to reject the notion that I was being lured into a trap.

ꕥ

The bright morning, of course, banished my adolescent fantasies, and I found I was even to enjoy a good breakfast with the local version of eggs Benedict with avocado and Serrano ham with the usual poached egg and Hollandaise sauce. I was tempted by the *ensaimada* and took one back to my room to have with the instant coffee that would be no match for the *café amb llet* served in the dining room.

While I wanted to wander through the streets and make some impulse purchases, my meetings had generated a lot of work, so I spent the morning making calls, typing up my notes and developing plans.

When I looked at my watch, it was twenty-to-twelve and I had to rush to get ready to meet Montserrat.

As it happened, she was walking in the front door as I entered the lobby. I had settled my bill and left my suitcase at the desk, but took my briefcase with my laptop with me.

Montserrat offered her cheek as I greeted her.

"Would you like a drink or coffee here?" I asked.

"I brought the car and am parked out front," she said, indicating a metallic midnight blue Renault Vel Satis at the foot of the steps. "You can put your suitcase in the trunk."

Montserrat told me that it had the unattractive name of *bleu crepuscule nacre*, or twilight blue mother of pearl. It was one of the largest cars I'd ever seen, and I had to ask what it was as I had never seen one.

"They stopped making them over ten years ago," she said. "It was Ricard's father's. It only has fifteen thousand miles on it. I don't drive that much, as I said, but it's good to run it once in a while."

I sank into the soft seat and stretched my legs under the well-appointed dashboard as Montserrat pulled into the traffic.

"It's not far," she said.

We drove up the Rambla de Catalunya then cut over to Passeig de Gràcia. While I didn't know this area well, I knew enough from the satellite maps that it was the same grid pattern as the rest of the modern city. I was surprised, then, when we turned into a tree-line road with large old homes like those on the Avinguda de Tibidabo.

There were few cars and as we cruised slowly down the road, I could see small alleys going off on both sides and twisting in to the distance.

Montserrat turned the car in to the broad drive of a massive art nouveau confection.

"Is this where you live?" I asked, in amazement.

Montserrat laughed.

"I wish!" she exclaimed, with an expression I suspected she didn't use often.

"As you will see, there is a large garage and the owners let me keep the car there," she explained. "My house is just a short walk."

One of the garage doors opened with the touch of the remote control in the car, and once parked, we walked down the long drive and back onto the main road. There was a turning into a small street (no visible name, but I assumed it was the address I had been using for Christmas cards) and we walked along for several hundred feet. In that short distance, it had taken several turns and was gently arcing in another direction, seemingly designed to disorient pedestrians.

"Here we are," Montserrat said, stopping in front of a traditional tall, narrow, stone house that may have been built in the seventeenth or eighteenth century.

Similar houses were up and down the street and seemed to date from all periods from the late Mediaeval to the art nouveau. They were in various stages of maintenance from the impeccable to the near-derelict.

I looked up. The house was three windows wide and went up four or five floors. The street was too narrow to see the top. It had nineteenth century cast iron grillwork on the ground floor, a large balcony on the first, and Juliet balconies above that.

"This is just like the Gothic Quarter used to be," I said. "It's wonderful to see something like this still exists."

Montserrat smiled.

"I'm glad you appreciate it. We can have a walk around after lunch."

She unlocked the carved oak door and we went into a small hallway. There was a door to the right and a staircase ahead of us. Switching on a light, she started up the stone stairs. The walls were blocks of stone that had been whitewashed at some stage but the covering was non-existent in many places. The staircase ended in a fairly large square hallway with a small table with dried flowers, lamps and candlesticks, two side chairs and several pictures on the walls.

Montserrat moved swiftly into the room at the front which was large and bright and had a square table set for lunch at the far end. As I stood in the middle of the room, looking around, she gave me a large glass of sherry.

"Benvingut a casa meva."

I guessed at the meaning.

"Thank you for your hospitality."

We drank and Montserrat moved to the table, and we sat down.

She indicated the bread, tomatoes, garlic and olive oil set out.

"You've been in Barcelona enough to know what to do," she said.

"Indeed," I said, proud to show off a little knowledge. "*Pa amb tomaquet* was one of the first things I was served here."

It's always a bit messy to eat and one's fingers smell of garlic, but it was delicious, especially with a glass of red wine poured from a crockery jug.

When we'd finished, Montserrat went to the kitchen. I asked if I could help, but she declined and told me where I could wash my hands.

"Just rinse them in cold water," she said. "Don't rub them together."

When I came back there was an assortment of salads on the table and Montserrat was coming in from the kitchen with plates of fish.

"*Peix de sant pere*," she announced, putting the plate before me.

I recognized the *poisson Saint Pierre*. Montserrat had grilled it and served it with pepper and lemon and, as I later tasted, a touch of garlic. She fetched a jug of chilled white wine from the kitchen and we began.

We talked about the food for a few moments, but Montserrat was not stupid.

"I can tell that you have many questions," she said, in the same warm manner that she had adopted at dinner. "Enjoy your meal and then we can talk. I will explain what I can."

As what I later saw as a preamble, Montserrat chatted about Spanish writers and artists.

"What many of them share is a sense of several levels of reality existing simultaneously," she said, talking about one of the writers. "Living memory only recently included those of the time before the Civil War and of the Civil War itself. Those stories and, more importantly, attitudes have been passed down the generations.

"We're losing what World War II memories there were, and, of course, there are still many around who remember Franco. Each of these eras has its contemporary associations and echoes."

Was this not true of all countries?

She also talked about Spanish and Catalan historians who had tried to write the truth about the Civil War, subsequent periods of unrest and the Catalan partisans, and how they differed in just about everything from the Basque separatists.

"Of course, every cause has its share of – "

"Extremists?"

"I was going to say, 'nut cases,'" she laughed, "but you get the idea."

She wasn't lecturing or preaching, but telling stories with bemusement.

"You see the layers of history – and layers of lives – are very different here than they were back in Pennsylvania," she concluded. "There were some layers, but people weren't aware of them like they are here."

We finished the meal and drank more wine.

"What's Nuria doing these days?" I asked.

"She's living in Florida doing something. She has two or three children that I haven't met. Her husband sells insurance. House, car or life, I don't know. I don't think she ever told me," she said, vaguely.

I hadn't meant to kick a sore spot. I had always thought them very close.

"Do you know," Montserrat resumed, "that when Ricard died, I had a picture postcard from Nuria. It was a picture of some alligators in the – you know, those swamps in Florida – "

"Everglades."

"That's it, everglades," she said, with a smile. "No one really knows where that name came from. Fields or grass, or river of grass? Who knows? Anyway, Nuria sent me a picture of some alligators in the everglades with, 'Very sorry to hear about your loss,' written on it."

She said this neutrally with no accusation nor any hint of sadness.

"I'm sorry," I said, knowing how feeble it sounded.

She smiled.

"You wrote a beautiful note," she said. "I had that instead."

Far from being an expert on such things, I suspected that Montserrat's behavior was a symptom of grief. She was living in an unhealthy time capsule and treating things with a nearly obsessive nature.

It was hard for me to hear about the extraordinary deterioration of her relationship with her sister. What had caused this tectonic shift? I refrained from asking as I had a flight to catch. Instead I tried a different tack.

"Were you able to get away after Ricard died?"

She looked at me as if my question was both intrusive and impertinent. I looked at my wine glass and drank some more.

After a moment, Montserrat replied.

"The best I could do was to just get on with my job," she said, softly. "I told you, Ricard was away a lot. Being on my own was not unusual. Things just continued."

I shook my head, sadly.

"It's good to go away to let the bruises heal," I said. "To plan what comes next, and see that life can go on. Even a week or two – "

"No. Not for me," she said, firmly. "I can't get away, besides, Isaac wouldn't like it."

"Isaac?"

"The man I work for at the library. I told you."

Montserrat was sounding impatient, so I didn't push it any further.

She stood up and went for her coat.

"Let's go for a walk before you have to head back."

I thought we'd go further down her street, into the unknown area, but we walked back to the main road.

I don't know if was then, or shortly after, that I began to get an inkling of what was to come.

The road wasn't as busy as it was when we had first come down it. The trees seemed to be taller with their branches overhanging the street.

There were still the large houses, but I thought I had remembered more modern buildings, but I may not have been paying attention.

We walked the few hundred yards to the intersection with Passeig de Gràcia, and it looked little different to the street we'd just walked down. There was little traffic, and looking up and down, I could see none of the modern buildings. Shops had neatly painted signs, and wares set out on the pavement.

We walked on, but I am sure Montserrat felt hesitation in my gait. There were more people about and I became aware of more details: the cast iron street lights, the names on the shops, the goods on display, the noise of the carts on the cobblestones, and tangle of wires on the telephone poles.

It was like seeing through a theatrical curtain – a scrim – where, when the lights come up behind it a new dimension of scenery and action can be seen. In this dream-like vision, traces of the twentieth-first century melted away. There were cars but they were all black and seemed to come from the twenties and thirties and clothing styles merged into non-descript forms. While there was still color, it was like stepping into a black and white film.

"What am I seeing, Montserrat?" I asked, not fully certain of what I saw. "I didn't think I drank that much."

The joke was a feeble attempt to cling to reality.

She gave me a gentle smile.

"When did you first notice?"

"Last night, on the way to the restaurant," I replied. "I thought I knew that street, but it's not what I saw."

Montserrat said nothing for a moment and we walked on.

The more I looked, the more detail I took in. I was seeing buildings and people gradually emerge like the phantom images on over-used video tapes. What surprised me most was that, as bizarre as this was, fascination subdued fear, and I watched the scene emerge with no sense of danger.

I stopped walking and simply watched as the scene composed itself. When a tram rolled by, all I could do was gape and laugh.

"Is this real?" I asked, turning to Montserrat. "What am I seeing?"

"It's unnerving, isn't it," she said. "You are seeing the city as it really is; its essence; its soul."

"But is it real?" I persisted.

Montserrat laughed loudly and briefly put her arm around me as we walked.

"You ask that in the home of surrealism?" she said, still laughing. "Reality is overrated. What you see isn't the past, nor yet is it fully the present."

Was this a way of seeing what had always existed – by certain people, in other places, at other times? It seemed a trick, or sleight of hand that you couldn't fathom until someone showed you.

That didn't make understanding what I was seeing any more comprehensible, in the way that even when you knew how a trick was done, you still couldn't do it.

With these streets and buildings, you didn't see them until you did, and then you saw them everywhere.

I looked at Montserrat, wondering. Had she lifted this veil, or had I done it myself? Or, did the city do it?

Montserrat walked easily, contented. I watched her face as she gazed down the road. She sensed I was staring at her and turned to me, smiling, almost beatifically.

She put her arm through mine again, and we turned to walk back to the house.

Still struggling to process what I had seen and what I failed to comprehend, my mind continued to race.

Montserrat unlocked the heavy door with the ancient key and went up the steps. As she hung up her coat, I moved to the window and looked into the street. She joined me in a moment, and we stood in her front room and continued looking out on to the world.

I don't know what Montserrat was thinking, but I was wondering what might come next. As if reading my mind, she replied to my half-formed thought.

"I told you, I couldn't get away," she said, gently, taking my hand. Then she leaned forward, lightly kissed my cheek and said, "and the truth of the matter is, *amor meu*, neither can you."

By the same author:

The Trumbull Chronicles

Fourscore and Upward
The Time of No Horizon
In an Age without Honor

Stories

Undivulged Crimes
Thoughts and Whispers

Novels

Ardmore Endings
The Rock Pool
Lost Lady
On the Edge of Dreams and Nightmares
The Countess Comes Home
Entrusted in Confidence
Portland Place: A novel of the time of Jane Austen
The Camels of the Qur'an
Wachusett
Nantucket Summer

Lattimer & Co.

Lattimer & Co. was established in Philadelphia in 1870 by "Colonel" Jonas Lattimer. The company now includes the imprints of Defarge Frères and Éditions Chaillot, both of Paris.

Printed in Great Britain
by Amazon